bank robbery!

Spencer Family Mysteries

Michael J. Rayes

RAFKA PRESS

This is a work of fiction. All names, characters, places, and events depicted herein are fictitious. Any resemblance to actual locales, events, or persons living or dead is purely coincidental.

Copyright © 2007 Michael J. Rayes
Illustrated by Laura Rayes
Illustrations copyright © 2006 Laura Rayes

All rights reserved. No part of this book may be reproduced or transmitted in any form or by any means, electronic or mechanical, including photocopying, recording, or by any information storage or retrieval system now existing or to be invented, without written permission from the author, except for the inclusion of brief quotations in a review.

Published by Rafka Press LLC
PO Box 8099
Phoenix, Ariz. 85066

ISBN-13: 978-0-9779628-0-8

10 9 8 7 6 5 4 3 2

First Edition
Printed in the United States of America

SPENCER FAMILY MYSTERIES and RAFKA PRESS are
Trademarks (TM 2006) of Rafka Press LLC

Library of Congress Control Number: 2006930432

Visit us online at www.rafkapress.com
For more information: info@rafkapress.com

dedication

To restless children everywhere —
especially my own.

"We're getting shot at!" the pilot screamed.

Tom and Rick grabbed the seats in front of them. Their knuckles turned white and they could feel the pressure in their stomachs as the helicopter banked hard.

Something suspicious happens every time Tom and Rick go to Creekwater National Bank to investigate the recent robbery. Tom's uncle, the Reverend Father Paul Spencer, helps the boys unravel the mystery. But they still don't know who really robbed the bank. And why are shady characters inside the bank when it's supposed to be closed?

Tom, Rick, and Father Spencer use their wits — and prayer — to help the police demolish a criminal conspiracy. They plunge into an exciting adventure that catapults them to a conclusion they never expected.

contents

Chapter 1

the chase

"They're turning!"

Rick Kline shouted the warning to his friend, Tom Spencer. Tom and Rick were in Tom's Mustang GT convertible, an eight-year-old yellow car he bought with his father's help.

They spotted an older Chevrolet Caprice with patchy paint and were following it. The Caprice matched the description of the suspect car in last week's bank robbery.

Suddenly, the Caprice turned down a wide street and shot off like a rocket. Rick and Tom could hear the old car's V-8 engine as the vehicle accelerated hard through second gear.

Tom hit the gas. The Mustang's V-8 engine obeyed immediately, and Tom and Rick were pinned to their seats by the force of the powerful engine. They were eager to help the police catch the robbers and wanted to read the Caprice's license plate or maybe catch a glimpse of the driver.

Brown-haired Tom Spencer is 18 years old, tall, and lean. Although young, he is a good investigator. Rick Kline is also 18 and has brown hair, but he is a little huskier than Tom and not quite as tall. Tom and Rick recently graduated from the same

1

high school and will start college in the fall. Rick often helps Tom in his work.

"We're going 60 miles an hour now," said Tom. "I need to back off. The speed limit is 45."

"But the robbers!" Rick cried. Tom, however, wasn't interested in driving above the speed limit when the police could do that and have the equipment necessary to capture the robbers.

"We'll have to phone Chief Roswell again and tell him where the car is headed," Tom said as he eased off the accelerator.

Rick immediately hit the redial button on his cell phone. He told police chief Sam Roswell, of the Creekwater Police Department, about the suspect car. As Rick was talking on the phone the suspect car got further and further ahead. The driver went through a yellow light.

The light changed, and Tom stopped. When the light turned green, Tom looked both ways and rapidly accelerated.

The suspect car was gone!

Tom turned the car around and drove home. The boys were eager to tell Tom's father about their adventure. Mr. John Spencer, full-time technology manager and part-time private investigator, was interested.

"How do you know, boys," Mr. Spencer said, "that this car was the same one used in the bank robbery?"

"Because, Dad," Tom replied, "it was a late '80s Chevy Caprice with blue peeling paint."

"Yeah," said Rick, "and why else would the driver try to get away so fast?"

"Well," Mr. Spencer replied, "I'm glad you found this out and told Chief Roswell. In fact, I just got off the phone with him."

"Oh, does he want your help with the robbery?" Tom asked excitedly.

"That's right," Mr. Spencer smiled. "And it's hungry work. How about some lunch?"

"Yes, it's about lunchtime," Mrs. Spencer added.

"Right on!" the boys exclaimed.

Mrs. Catherine Spencer is average height and has medium brown hair with a touch of gray. She is very healthy and likes gardening. She worries about her sons, but she is proud of them, especially Tom.

Mrs. Spencer brought out lunchmeat and sandwich rolls and prepared the sandwiches. Mr. Spencer took out the plates and handed them to Tom and Rick, and the boys helped set the table. Soon they were all feasting on turkey and roast beef sandwiches, potato salad from last night's dinner, and fruit punch.

Over lunch, they discussed the case. Last week, Creekwater National Bank was robbed by more than one person. In the middle of the night the robbers entered through the roof and stole more than half a million dollars in cash.

The video cameras had been disabled and the alarm system was turned off. A security guard at an office across the street saw a 1980s model Chevrolet Caprice, with patchy blue paint, at the bank. He saw the open car trunk and people loading bags into it. Then the car drove off.

The guard was suspicious and called the police. It was too dark and the guard was too far away to see much detail.

Creekwater is a thriving, modern southwestern city of 400,000 people, and there hadn't been a bank robbery in almost two years.

"Did the guard see the people going through the roof?" Tom asked.

"No," his father answered. "The police found out about the roof when they arrived. They think it could be an inside job."

"An inside job!" Tom said. "You mean the bank's own employees robbed it?" Tom and Rick looked at each other.

"Maybe," Mr. Spencer answered. "But was it one employee or many? Or none at all?"

No one said anything for a minute. Finally, Tom spoke up.

"I'd sure like to talk to some of those bank employees."

"Oh, I don't know," Mrs. Spencer said. "That could be dangerous." Tom and Rick looked at each other and grinned. Mrs. Spencer sighed. "It seems like you boys are always getting yourselves into hot water!"

"Tell you what, boys," Mr. Spencer said. "Why don't you talk to that security guard first, and find out for yourselves what he knows? Maybe you'll learn something new. Then, we'll see about the bank employees."

"Okay, Dad!" Tom said. "Let's go!" Both boys got up and started for the door.

"Hold it!" Mrs. Spencer said. She looked down at the dishes on the table and slowly cleared her throat.

"And how do you know," Mr. Spencer asked, "which guard it is?"

"Oh, yeah," Tom mumbled. Both boys began clearing the lunch dishes, while Mr. Spencer continued speaking.

"You can get the name of the guard from Chief Roswell, but I need to check my e-mail anyway. I have the chief's address, so why don't we e-mail him?" Mr. Spencer said.

Tom agreed, and when the dishes were done, the boys followed Mr. Spencer to his den.

John Spencer had two computers, a police scanner, a ham radio, and a short-wave radio in his den. There were also several books. His desk had stacks of papers on it and a block of wood with four miniature brass clocks attached to it. Mr. Spencer made the set himself, each clock set to a different time zone.

Mr. Spencer opened his e-mail program and saw a message that read "To Spencer."

Spencer, back off bank case or else. We know where you live.

It was a threat!

Chapter 2

....

setting traps

"I don't believe my eyes!" Tom gasped as he read the e-mail threat.

No one said anything for a few moments. The three of them sat and stared at the computer screen.

"Now, isn't that interesting," Mr. Spencer said.

"Interesting!" Rick exclaimed. "Mr. Spencer, you could be in danger!"

"No, I mean it's interesting that I only just started this case. Someone already knows that I'm looking into it."

Mr. Spencer forwarded the message to Chief Roswell. The message was from 123456@xacmegomail.com.

"Isn't X Acme Go Mail one of those anonymous web e-mail accounts?" Rick asked.

"Yes, it is," Mr. Spencer answered. Then, in his message to Chief Roswell, he typed:

Sam,
Can you trace address of attached message?
John Spencer

Mr. Spencer also sent another message asking about the guard's name. Suddenly, he stood up.

"Come on, boys. Let's go for a walk."

"A walk?" Tom asked. Mr. Spencer winked at him as if to say he was up to something. Tom and Rick grinned, and they went outside.

They walked past four houses on their street and didn't say anything. Finally, Mr. Spencer spoke up.

"A bit hot out."

"Dad, come on!" Tom pleaded. "What are we doing out here?"

"All right, here's the thing," Mr. Spencer replied. "Someone knows I'm on the case, but it's only been a few hours since the chief put me on it. Someone could have overheard our phone conversation."

They walked around the corner. Mr. Spencer and Tom waved to a neighbor watering her lawn.

"We don't know," Mr. Spencer continued, "if the phones are bugged, or if someone bugged the house somehow. So we need to set a couple of traps."

"All right!" Tom said. "We're with you!" Tom and Rick extended their thumbs to show they agreed. They continued down the next street.

"For the house trap," Mr. Spencer continued, "you boys can pretend you took a picture of the people in the suspect car. When we get back to the house, tell me the picture and the camera are in your Mustang. Then, we'll see what happens."

"And if someone tries to steal that camera..." Rick started to say.

"We'll know there's a wireless microphone bug in the house!" Tom finished.

"Right," Mr. Spencer said. They rounded a corner and walked down the Spencer family's street again. A dog barked from behind a fence.

"What about the phone bug?" Tom asked.

"I'll take care of that," Mr. Spencer replied. "I'll talk to Uncle Paul about it." Tom's Uncle Paul is Mr. Spencer's older brother. He is known to everyone else as Father Paul Spencer, pastor of St. Anne's Catholic Church. The tall and lean Father Spencer shares his family's investigative talents. He helped Mr. Spencer on other cases in the past.

Mr. Spencer pressed a speed-dial button on his cell phone while they walked. They passed several more houses on their way home while Mr. Spencer talked with his brother, the priest. He finally ended the call.

"We're all set," Mr. Spencer said to Tom and Rick. "Uncle Paul and I will pretend I have some evidence."

"Wow!" said Rick. "That's sneaky!" Rick and Tom both laughed.

They arrived back at the Spencer house. Once inside, they went to the kitchen. Mr. Spencer looked at Rick and nodded silently. Rick smiled.

"Oh, uh, Mr. Spencer," Rick said loudly, "I forgot...er, I *didn't* tell you that we have a picture of the people in that Caprice we followed today. The camera is still in Tom's car."

The trap was set.

"Oh, okay," Mr. Spencer replied. He then went upstairs to his den. A few hours ago when Chief Roswell telephoned him about taking the case, Mr. Spencer was in the kitchen. If there was a hidden microphone bug in the kitchen, he wanted to talk upstairs.

Mr. Spencer telephoned Father Spencer and they exchanged greetings. Mr. Spencer continued speaking.

"That security guard told me they caught the men at the bank on videotape. I have a videotape in my car but it's the only copy. Want to watch it with me before I turn it in?" he pretended.

"Sure thing, John," the priest answered. "That should be very interesting to watch! I can come over tomorrow."

They ended the call. Mr. Spencer actually did have a video-tape in his car, but it was a movie.

"I'll have to visit Father Paul later this evening and explain the case a little more," Mr. Spencer thought to himself.

He turned toward his computer and checked his e-mail. He received a reply from Chief Roswell. The security guard's name is Brad Holmes, and he usually works at night. He is employed with Allied Security. Mr. Spencer walked downstairs and got a drink of water. He motioned to the boys, and began writing a note.

If burglar steals camera from your car, then house is bugged. If video in my car is stolen, then phone line is tapped.

Both boys smiled and gave a thumbs-up.

That night, Tom had trouble sleeping. He listened for the garage alarm or one of the car alarms to sound. He heard nothing.

The next morning, he ran downstairs and went to the garage.

Everything was okay. The camera was still in his car. He went to the kitchen.

"Thomas," said Mrs. Spencer, "your father said his car was okay this morning before he left for work."

"Okay, Mom. Thanks," Tom said.

The traps didn't work!

"Oh, he also said he would try to call Chief Roswell today at work if he has time," Mrs. Spencer added.

Tom's little brothers, Billy and Jason, entered the kitchen.

"Hiya, squirts!"

"Don't call me squirt!" Billy, 13, said in reply.

"Okay, Billy," Tom said.

"Don't call me Billy anymore either," Billy said. "Just call me Bill."

"My boys are all growing up!" Mrs. Spencer said. There are four Spencer children. Jason is 10. The only sister in the family, Michelle, is 15. She is helping her grandmother and spending a few nights at her house.

The sun was already warming the ground and there wasn't a cloud in the sky. The three brothers sat down to a breakfast of cold cereal and warm sunshine.

After breakfast, Tom telephoned Rick and told him the traps didn't work. They decided to talk to Father Spencer. Since Tom wanted to stay home and listen for a burglar last night, he didn't talk to the office security guard. Tom and Rick agreed to stay up late tonight and visit the guard.

Tom walked to the laundry room next to the kitchen. From the laundry room, a door led to the Spencer's attached garage. He went into the garage and got in his car to drive to Rick's. He pressed a button on his remote garage-door opener clipped to the car's sun visor to roll open the garage door.

He saw something move outside the door!

Tom sprang from his car and ran to the front of the garage. He heard something scrambling through a shrub around the corner! He carefully stepped around the corner to the side of the garage.

"Who — who's there?" Tom called. He stepped forward near the shrub. He looked all around the leaves and walked closer.

Suddenly, the bottom of the shrub shook! Tom gasped. A brown cat ran out of the bush.

"Darned cat!" Tom sighed. He walked back to the garage and started his Mustang. The powerful engine roared awake and then purred quietly. He drove to Rick's house and picked up Rick. Together they drove to St. Anne's. They told Tom's Uncle Paul about the car chase and the traps.

"That's odd," Father Spencer said. "If the bank robbers got away with so many thousands of dollars, why would they still drive that old car?"

"We were hoping you would know," Rick said.

"And the traps you set didn't work," Father Spencer added, "although it's only been one day."

No one said anything.

"It's turning into a big mystery," Tom finally said.

"This could mean that someone at the police station is part of the robbery," Father Spencer said. "Or someone at the bank! I spoke with Chief Roswell this morning. He told the bank managers right away that your father is on the case."

"That means," said Rick, "the only one who could have threatened Mr. Spencer is someone at the bank or a policeman!"

"Oh, I hope it's not a policeman!" Tom said. Rick put his elbows on his knees and sank his chin into his hands. Father Spencer rubbed his forehead.

The phone rang. Mr. Spencer was calling. He first called the Spencer house, and Mrs. Spencer told him Tom and Rick were visiting Father Spencer. The priest gave Tom the phone. His father told him some exciting news.

The police found the suspect car!

Chapter 3

burning the evidence

Tom learned the suspect car's location from his father and hung up the phone. Tom, Rick, and Father Spencer piled into Tom's Mustang and drove north. While they drove, Tom explained the details to his uncle and Rick.

"The police had three different calls this morning to report the car. Farmers in the area could see the smoke for miles."

"Smoke?" Rick asked.

"Yeah," Tom answered, "the car was abandoned out in the wilderness and burned."

"Burned!" Rick exclaimed.

"Oh, my," Father Spencer said.

They drove several miles and the city gradually faded away behind them. They drove north on the highway five more miles.

"There's the signpost," Tom noted. "Mile 173."

"Ah, there they are," Rick said. Tom turned down a bumpy dirt road and saw his father's car, a squad car, and the burned-out Caprice. Mr. Spencer and two policemen were standing behind a line of police tape that read *Crime Scene — Do Not Cross.*

"What a sight!"

The two amateur sleuths and the priest said hello to Tom's father. Mr. Spencer introduced them to the two policemen. One of the officers lifted up the police tape and the three walked under it.

Rick whistled. "What a sight!" The car body was so black, they couldn't tell what color it once was. All four tires were flat. The dashboard had melted so badly, they couldn't tell the speedometer from the gas gauge.

"The tires exploded from the heat, huh?" Rick asked.

"That's what it looks like," Father Spencer replied. Mr. Spencer and the two policemen nodded.

"Have you found any evidence?" Tom asked.

"Well, there's..." one of the officers started to say. Mr. Spencer held up his hand and smiled at the officer.

"Why don't you boys take a look around the car?" Mr. Spencer suggested. Rick and Tom smiled and walked toward the open trunk. Father Spencer stood in front of the car and rubbed his chin.

A tire jack was inside the trunk. The jack had dried mud on it. There was also a spare tire that still had some air and a half-melted plastic soft-drink bottle. The boys walked around the car. The fire did more damage to the front of the car than the rear. There was still water under the Caprice from the fire department. The tires and wheel wells were wet. There was nothing noticeable inside the car. The seats were blackened and the boys could see the wire frames where the cushions burned away. Rick leaned into the car.

"Smells terrible!" Rick exclaimed.

"That's burnt plastic!" said one of the policemen. "Try not to breathe it."

"Say, Dad," Tom said to his father, "the jack still has mud on it. Looks like the firemen didn't soak it."

"Bingo!" said Mr. Spencer. "And what does the mud tell you?" Father Spencer walked around to the trunk and examined the jack.

"The guy changed the tire out in the country, and not in the city!" Tom shouted.

"Yeah, because he was probably on a dirt road!" Rick added.

"That's right, boys," Mr. Spencer said. "We don't know if that was a special trip, or if the driver lives in the country."

"We're investigating that," added the officer standing next to Mr. Spencer.

Father Spencer spoke up. "John, can we get the addresses of all the bank employees?" The priest wanted to find out which employees lived in the country.

"Yes, actually," Mr. Spencer replied, "I should receive a fax from Chief Roswell later today. I'll make you a copy."

"Your uncle and your father think alike!" Rick said to Tom. Everyone laughed.

"Well, gentlemen," Mr. Spencer said, "I need to get back to the office." He walked toward his car. Father Spencer motioned to Tom and Rick, and the three said goodbye to the two policemen. The trio of amateur sleuths followed Mr. Spencer to his car.

"John," the priest said in a low voice, "have you found out anything about that e-mail threat?"

"Yes," Mr. Spencer answered, "it came from a library patron so it could have been anyone."

"Library patron?" Tom asked.

"Yup, Chief Roswell's men traced the e-mail to a computer 'IP' address. The IP address is for the Creekwater Library System's firewall server. Someone used a library computer terminal, logged on to the anonymous X Acme Go Mail service, and sent me the threat." Mr. Spencer answered.

"But can't the library trace it to the right terminal?" Rick asked.

"Maybe they could," Mr. Spencer said, "but hundreds of people use the library. We still don't have a clue who did it."

"A dead end," Father Spencer sighed.

The wind picked up a bit. The small desert bushes waved in the breeze. The strong smell of burnt plastic and metal blew over. Tom scrunched up his face.

"So," Father Spencer continued, "we know those traps didn't work. No one bugged your house or your phone. And whoever sent the threat did it anonymously. But it must have been..." Father Spencer stopped talking and looked over his shoulder at the two policemen several yards away, who were putting the muddy jack in the squad car.

"It must have been," the priest whispered, "a policeman or a bank employee. No one else knew you were on the case at the time of the threat."

"Yes, that's right," Mr. Spencer said. "I'm working with the Creekwater police, so I'll investigate them myself." Mr. Spencer then looked at the boys. "Can you boys talk to some of the bank employees after we get that fax?"

"Sure!" Tom said. "Yeah!" Rick added.

"The only thing," Mr. Spencer said, holding up both his hands, "I want your Uncle Paul to go with you, Tom. I don't want you talking to them alone."

"Yes," Father Spencer agreed. "I'd like to go with you. It could be dangerous if it's an inside job."

"Okay, Dad. Okay, Uncle Paul," Tom said. "Oh, we still need to talk to that security guard tonight."

Mr. Spencer said goodbye and drove toward town.

"Can you boys drop me off at the rectory?" Father Spencer asked. "I have some work to do for the parish school. Tom, I'll call you when I get that fax from your father."

"Sure, Uncle Paul," Tom replied. The three of them piled into Tom's Mustang and headed back to the city. Tom drove the priest to the church. Tom and Rick went to O'Sullivan's, a local burger shop, for lunch. They said hello to Sean, their friend from school who works at O'Sullivan's.

Tom ordered a double hamburger, fries, and a chocolate shake. Rick ordered a quarter-pound bacon hamburger with fries and a soda. The boys sat down to enjoy their meals.

"Man, I'm hungry," Tom said.

"Ummpf, me too," Rick answered between gulps.

After lunch, they drove to Rick's house. The Kline residence is a sprawling single-level ranch house. The boys were listening to music on Rick's radio when Tom's cell phone rang.

"Hello?" Tom said into the phone. "Hi, Uncle Paul! Great. Okay. We'll see you in a few minutes."

Father Spencer received the faxed list of bank employees' addresses!

Tom and Rick drove to St. Anne's and picked up Father Spencer. They discussed the list as Tom drove to the Creekwater Bank.

"There is only one address on here that's even close to the city limits, where the dirt roads are," Father Spencer said. "Christine Travinski is the name on the list."

When they pulled up to the bank, the trio got out of the car and looked at the bank building. Rick looked up and noticed some large pieces of plywood and wood boards attached to the roof.

"Must be where the robbers broke in," Rick said, pointing to the wood.

"Looks like the wood is a temporary fix until they seal the roof," the priest added.

The three of them entered the bank and introduced themselves. David Switzer, the vice-president, explained that he would help them because the bank president was busy. They went to Switzer's office in the back of the bank. The priest, usually quiet around others, spoke up and explained their mission. He told Switzer that they are related to John Spencer, the detective.

"We would like to talk with some employees, too," Father Spencer added.

"No problem," Switzer said, smiling. "Help yourself. The sooner we get to the bottom of this, the better," he continued in a thick New England accent.

The boys followed the priest out of Switzer's office and spoke to several employees. They talked to each bank teller and loan officer. One loan officer, Bob Taylor, was a short, medium-built man. He had dark hair. He quickly became angry.

"I already told the cops I don't know anything!" Taylor growled. "Why don't you three just buzz off?"

"We're only trying to help the bank!" Tom exclaimed.

"If you really want to help the bank, then leave me alone so I can finish this paperwork," Taylor snarled.

The sleuthing trio also talked to Christine Travinski and discovered she is a bank teller. After asking a few questions, Father Spencer mentioned his car.

"I had to change the battery last month," he remarked. "But I'd rather do that than change a tire!"

"Oh, I don't even know how to change a tire," Miss Travinski giggled. "I'm afraid I wouldn't even know where to look for the car battery."

The two boys and the priest finished their conversation and left the bank.

Back at the priest's rectory, the trio snacked on cranberry juice and cookies. Rick gulped the juice and was noisier than Tom and Father Spencer combined. By the time Tom drank half his juice, Rick's juice glass was almost empty.

"Well," Father Spencer said between sips of juice, "we certainly didn't learn as much as I thought we would."

"Really?" Rick asked. "I thought we found out a lot! That angry Mr. Taylor, for one thing!"

"Yeah, he's got to have something to do with it!" Tom added.

"Perhaps," the priest said. "Or perhaps he is simply tired of answering questions."

The three thought about the case while they finished the package of cookies.

"Tom," Father Spencer said, "do you know why I brought up car repairs with Miss Travinski?"

"Yeah," Tom replied. "To see if she knows how to change a tire."

"Then maybe *she* was the one who used that muddy jack in the suspect car," Rick added.

"Very good, boys," the priest said. "But I believe Miss Travinski. I could be wrong, but I don't think she had anything to do with that car."

"Hmm," Rick said, "I see what you mean. We really didn't get any leads at the bank."

"Let's go back tomorrow," Father Spencer suggested. "Maybe we'll learn more."

Rick stood up and brushed the cookie crumbs from his shirt into the palm of his hand. He walked to the priest's garbage can and briskly wiped both his hands over it.

"Good as new!" Rick said to the two grinning Spencers.

"He cleans up pretty nicely, doesn't he?" Father Spencer said to Tom. The priest winked at Rick while Tom chuckled.

"Yeah, not too bad!" Tom laughed.

That night, Tom and Rick went to the office near the bank. Brad Holmes, the security guard, was there.

"I sure wish I could accommodate y'all with some refreshments, but I'm afraid I can't leave muh post here," Holmes said in a heavy Southern drawl.

"Oh, that's okay," Tom replied. The boys asked him about the suspect car.

"Well," Holmes answered, "it's like I told the city police. There was three of 'em, I reckon, loadin' up that old car. Huh! Sort of like my old jalopy, what with the peelin' paint and all. 'Course, it was dark and I couldn't see 'pert near much o' anything, dadburnit. Sometimes I wonder why they used that old car. My old Fairmont sure don't have the git-up-an-go it used to. Why, just the other day, the garage told me not only is the engine all gummed up, but I'll need a new fuel pump directly! And then I was..."

"Um, Mr. Holmes," Tom interrupted, "did you notice anything about those three men? Did you hear their voices?"

"Oh, uh, no, sure didn't," Holmes replied. "Was too far away to catch any of their jaws flappin'. And it was too dark to see much.

By the time I called our city's fine police force, they was high-tailin' it out o' there faster than a young racoon during huntin' season!"

The boys thanked Mr. Holmes for his help. They drove to their houses and went to their beds, where a good night's sleep refreshed them both.

The next day, Tom and Rick picked up Father Spencer. They drove to the bank. The sleuthing trio spoke with Mr. Switzer again.

"I'm surprised to see you again so soon. Find anything out?" Switzer asked.

"No, nothing big," Father Spencer replied. "But we wanted to ask you about your bank's security." The priest leaned forward. "I know the building has security alarms. But don't most banks have security measures for the money, too?" he asked.

"Yes," Switzer answered. "We use everything from the serial numbers to disappearing ink on the uncirculated bills."

"Then why don't we just trace the stolen money?" Rick immediately asked.

"Well, young man," Mr. Switzer answered, "the bags of money that were stolen were very new. We don't have a lot of employees right now, and that money was stolen before we had time to secure it!"

Tom and Rick both groaned.

The priest and the vice-president discussed the case for a few minutes. The three amateur sleuths finally got up to leave, when Father Spencer turned toward Switzer's desk.

"Looks like payroll sheets you have there," Father Spencer said, pointing to some printouts on Switzer's desk. "Do vice-presidents handle payroll?"

"Uh, no, actually," Mr. Switzer said, frowning. "Like I said before, we are short on staff, so some of us are doing extra work."

The three amateur sleuths drove away from the bank. What they did not notice, however, was the gray sedan that was following them.

Tom and Rick talked about the bank robbery with Father Spencer. They also discussed the weather, their families, and school. They enjoyed the peaceful, sunny afternoon as they talked and laughed.

Meanwhile, a tall man in dark sunglasses drove the gray sedan about two hundred feet behind the trio and followed their every turn.

It did not look like the peaceful day would stay that way for long.

Chapter 4

the knife

Tom drove the car to a convenience store and he, Rick, and Father Spencer bought some drinks. The man in the gray sedan parked near Tom's Mustang.

When the three sleuths came out of the store, they gasped.

A knife was stuck in the driver's seat of Tom's car!

A note was stuck to the blade of the knife. Rick quickly looked around. There was only one other car, and it belonged to a customer inside the store.

No one else was around.

"Oh, man!" Tom cried. Father Spencer sighed heavily. Rick ran inside the store and asked the clerk and the customer if they saw anything. They both said no.

Tom stared at the knife until Rick came back from the store.

"No one saw anything," Rick said. "Aren't you going to read the note?"

Tom bit his lower lip. "I guess." He took a handkerchief from his pocket and used it to pull the knife out. He had to wriggle the knife up and down, since it was pushed into the seat so hard!

While still holding the knife handle, Tom slowly pulled the paper off the blade.

"Don't cut yourself, Thomas," Father Spencer cautioned.

Tom unfolded the paper and read the note out loud.

Spencers, back off before someone gets hurt.

Rick tapped his right fist into his left hand and began pacing. Father Spencer rubbed his chin. Tom leaned on the trunk of his car. He put his hand on his forehead with his eyes closed. Finally Father Spencer spoke up.

"Tom, your father and I went to school with a man who runs an upholstery shop. He can fix that seat." The priest put his hand on Tom's shoulder. "Don't worry about it now. Let's call the police."

"Yeah, I suppose," Tom sighed. Then, he grew angry. "Yeah! I'll call them myself." He used his cell phone to call Chief Roswell. Father Spencer walked inside the store and asked the clerk if they had an outside surveillance camera to capture criminal activity on tape. The clerk told him they only have an inside camera.

Tom wanted to use the fingerprinting kit in the trunk of his car to dust the knife for prints. Chief Roswell asked him not to use it, because the chief wanted his officers to do the fingerprinting. Tom finished reporting the damage and the threat and said goodbye to the chief.

The three amateur sleuths stood around the Mustang, looking at the knife for a few minutes while they waited for the police to arrive.

The knife was a cheap buck-style folding knife with a four-inch blade. The handle was worn and rusty in parts.

"Whoever did this," Tom said to Rick and Father Spencer, "didn't want to waste a good knife."

Rick spoke up. "I'd sure like to find him!"

"We may not have to wait long to start searching," said Father Spencer. "Here come the police." A squad car with lights flashing pulled into the parking lot. Rick waved toward the car.

When the policeman got out of his car, the boys told him what happened. They gave him the knife and the note.

"I'll take these back to our lab downtown. They can analyze them there," the officer said.

"Do you know when we'll get the results?" asked Father Spencer.

"They're pretty good there. Shouldn't be more than a day or two. In the meantime, Tom, keep this form. It has the police report number on it. You may need it later."

The three sleuths thanked the officer. He put the knife and the note in a plastic bag and put the bag in his trunk. As the officer drove off, Tom and Rick looked at Father Spencer.

"Well, boys," Father Spencer said, "I think we need to talk to both your parents about this. Tom, your dad really needs to know, but Rick, I think we should tell your mom and dad about this incident. They need to know about it."

"Do you think they'll try to stop you from hanging around with me?" Tom asked.

"Nah. I'm 18 now, man! Besides, they trust all you Spencers."

"Eighteen or not," Father Spencer replied, "you still live with your parents and you still have responsibilities." The priest fumbled with his cell phone. "May I have your phone number?" Father Spencer smiled.

"Sure. Here, I'll speed-dial my house and you can use my phone. Here you go, Father, it's ringing."

The priest took the phone and began speaking. "Hello, Mrs. Kline? This is Father Spencer from Saint Anne's. Very well, thank you, and yourself? Wonderful! Mrs. Kline, Rick is here with me… oh, he's perfectly fine. But I need to tell you about something that happened this morning…"

While Father Spencer talked with Rick's mother on the phone, Tom and Rick discussed the case.

"I think we should talk to that grumpy Taylor at the bank again," Tom said.

"Yeah. But I don't know how talkative he'll be."

"He's not like that security guard, that's for sure!" Tom answered.

"Now, there's a guy who's pretty talkative. And helpful." Tom's eyes widened and he took a big, quick breath.

"I know!" Tom exclaimed. "We'll follow the guy around, and see what he's up to!" Rick smiled and showed a thumbs-up.

Father Spencer finished his conversation and returned the telephone to Rick.

"I told your mother about the knife in Tom's car. She is worried, but she trusts us to be careful, like you said. I told her we called the police about it."

"Thanks, Father. I'm glad you told Mom instead of me. Sometimes, it just all comes out wrong when I try to tell her stuff," Rick said.

"No problem," Father said, smiling. "She seems like a pretty caring person."

"Yes, she is."

"Where to now, Uncle Paul?" Tom asked. "Should we take you to the rectory?"

"Yes, please," the priest answered while glancing at his watch. "I do need to get back. I'll call your father while I'm there."

That afternoon, Tom and Rick waited in the car across the street from the bank.

"It's after five o'clock," Rick said. "Wonder when Taylor will get out of there." He muffled a long yawn.

"Beats me. I thought everyone left right about now. Look, some people are leaving…"

Three bank employees walked to their cars. A few minutes later, two more employees left. Finally, Tom and Rick saw Bob Taylor leave the building and walk toward a red minivan.

Less than a minute later, a red minivan and a yellow Mustang were driving on the freeway. The minivan exited the freeway, turned into a neighborhood of neat houses, and pulled into a driveway. Tom and Rick parked a block away.

"Well, *that* was exciting," Rick fumed. "This guy is boring."

"Yeah, no action here. At least not today, anyway."

The boys spent the rest of the week following Taylor and learning about Creekwater National Bank. They also learned that the police lab did not find any prints or other clues on the knife that was stuck in Tom's car. The knife was clean!

Friday night, Tom had dinner at home with his family as usual. He discussed the case with his father at the dinner table.

"We didn't find out anything about that Taylor fellow," Tom said between bites of green beans. "I thought it would be fun to find out what his connection is to the case. But we're both getting tired of following him."

"Well, Tom," Mr. Spencer grinned, "you're discovering that detective work can be tedious. It's not like those TV shows."

"What TV shows?" Tom's little brother Jason asked.

"You know, TV shows about cops and stuff," Billy answered.

"One more thing," Mr. Spencer added, "you and Rick are following Mr. Taylor because of his outburst at the bank, right? Is that your only lead?"

"Yeah, I guess so," Tom sighed. He took a drink from his glass. "Maybe we should investigate a little more. The bank is closed tomorrow, so we'll look at the building again since there won't be so many people there."

"Please pass the potatoes," Mrs. Spencer said. Mr. Spencer handed her the bowl.

"Anything for you, dear," he said, smiling.

"Aw, sheesh! That's not what you said to me when I wanted the meatloaf!" Billy grumbled.

"Well now, cheer up when you ask for — and I mean ask for, not demand — the meatloaf, and you might get a nice answer. Learn how to be polite," his father answered. Mrs. Spencer glared at Billy, but he pretended not to notice.

"Oh, Tom, I wanted to let you know," Mr. Spencer said, "Chief Roswell and I did a bit of research this week. When you and Rick saw that suspect car, we think whoever drove it was trying to get rid of it. That's why they eventually burned it."

"That makes sense! They can afford to get rid of it since they have all that stolen bank money."

"Yes," Mr. Spencer answered. "And I've been looking at the police department on my own. I can't find any evidence of an inside job so far. At least not at the police department."

"That's a relief!" Mrs. Spencer said.

"But it could still be an inside job by a bank employee, right, Dad?" Tom asked.

"It probably is. I don't see how else someone could have known exactly where to cut the roof to get into the safe."

Mr. Spencer drank the rest of his wine.

"I'll work with the chief a lot more next week, and I'll see what we can come up with. Tom, let me know if you and Uncle Paul come up with anything, okay? You've grown up so much, but I don't want you getting hurt."

"Okay Dad. Don't worry! I'll be careful."

Chapter 5

caught spying

The next morning, Rick drove his father's pickup truck to the Spencer family's house. Mr. Kline bought the truck a few years ago as a second vehicle for hauling home-improvement and gardening supplies. Even though all the windows were closed in the Spencer house, everyone heard Rick drive up. The truck is 14 years old, but the holes in the muffler are a little newer than that. The truck's engine knocked and pinged while the exhaust system barked loudly and sputtered.

"I think she's burning a little rich on the fuel!" Rick yelled over the engine noise.

"Man, I forgot this old truck was such a beater," Tom yelled back as he briskly walked toward the truck.

"Well, it's not as nice as your pretty little yellow pony car, that's for sure."

"Yeah but look, my car only has one color of paint," Tom answered while pointing to the blotches of primer on the door, the blue body, and brown tailgate. "This truck has three!"

"Ok, mister wise-guy, hop in!"

Tom slid onto the vinyl bench seat. There was a large crack in the seat between the two boys, and a few greasy wires hung down underneath the dashboard.

"Thanks for driving while my car is in the shop," Tom said.

"Ah, no problem."

Rick drove on the freeway with the palm of his hand resting on the steering wheel. His window was rolled all the way down, and his left arm rested on the door with his elbow hanging out of the truck. Tom's window was rolled all the way up. The speedometer needle hovered on top of the 70 mark.

"Speed limit's 55 here, watch out!" Tom yelled over the wind and engine noise.

"Huh?" Rick looked at Tom.

"The speed limit is 55!"

Rick scrunched up his nose. "Whatever."

After a couple more miles, Rick exited the freeway and turned down 42nd Street. Rick slowed the truck to turn into the bank parking lot.

"Rick!" Tom gasped. "Keep driving!"

Rick learned over the years to trust Tom's judgement about investigations. He gradually accelerated and passed the bank without asking Tom for an explanation. They drove past an empty field and an office building.

"You want to tell me why we didn't pull into the bank now?" Rick asked.

"I saw a car there. I think there was a light on in the back of the bank. I needed time to think before we pulled in."

Rick bit his lower lip. He pulled into an office parking lot and parked the truck.

"If you want to go back to the bank, I can park away from it and I'll kill the engine so they don't hear us," Rick said.

"Yeah, let's do it," Tom answered. Rick pulled out of the parking lot and drove toward the bank. He passed the bank and turned into the far side of an office building next to the bank. As the truck rolled past the row of office suites, Rick gently bumped the gearshift into neutral and turned off the ignition. The truck rolled to a stop near some garbage dumpsters behind the office building.

"This is good," Tom said. "We can't see the bank from here, so whoever is in there can't see us." Both boys got out of the truck. Rick began taking some equipment out of the truck cab, while Tom walked past the dumpsters. He could see the bank once he stood on the other side of the dumpsters. He stared at the bank building for a few seconds before he turned around and walked back to the truck.

"I'll take this side," Tom said. Then he pointed toward the bank. "Can you go over to the other side and look in the windows?"

Rick showed a thumbs-up. Both boys clipped their two-way radios to their belts. Tom carried a spy-listening kit with him, which consisted of a box about the size of a small CD player, a suction cup with a wire connected to the box, and a set of headphones.

"Let's meet back here at the truck," Tom said.

Tom and Rick slowly walked toward the bank building. Even though it was still morning, they could feel the summer sun's intense heat. Rick squinted his eyes. Tom began to sweat. He noticed the eerie silence and that there weren't many cars driving on 42nd Street that morning.

A couple of black birds began squawking in a tree above them as they walked under it.

The bank loomed larger as they walked closer to it. Rick walked away from Tom, toward the far side of the bank's southern parking lot. Tom walked toward the other side of the building, away from the window with the light shining in it. He heard the faint whoosh sound of a car approaching. The whoosh gradually got louder. He ducked behind a bush, grabbed his radio, and clicked the button.

"Car coming!" Tom said into the radio in a hoarse whisper.

"Gotcha," Rick answered into his radio. He stopped walking. He was at the rear of the building, so the driver of the car wouldn't see him. The whoosh got louder as the car sped past the bank.

Tom crouched down and put the suction cup
from his spy kit on the glass.

"All clear, no big deal," Tom said into his radio.

"No problem," came the reply from the radio's speaker. Tom stood up and began walking again. Sweat dripped from his forehead as he walked to the side of the building. He quickly glanced through a window but didn't see anyone. He crouched down and put the suction cup from his spy kit on the glass. The spy kit can pick up human voices from a quarter-mile away. He put the headphones over his head and turned up the sensitivity knob on the kit, then the volume knob. He could hear a man's voice from somewhere inside the bank!

"I don't know. When we… the parts… as long as you remember to clean them up before you ship them out this time…"

"Wait! What's that?" Tom heard another man's voice say.

"What! Hey! Who's that looking in the window? We got to get him!"

"Right! We'll find out why he's nosing around!"

Tom felt a chill go down his back. He quickly looked up into the window but still didn't see anyone inside.

"They must have seen Rick looking in a window on the other side!" Tom thought.

A man with a black shirt hurried outside and ran quietly toward Rick, who didn't see him coming. Tom yanked his radio from his waist and was about to yell into it when he heard the man shouting. Tom pulled the suction cup off the window and ran away from the building as fast as he could.

"Hold it, you!" the man growled as he grabbed Rick's arm.

"Hey! Let go of me! What's going on!"

"That's what you'll have to tell me. Come inside."

The man pulled Rick into the building!

Once inside, they struggled past the rows of teller windows and shuffled toward the offices in back. The man finally let go of Rick.

"Walk into that office," the man pointed, "and don't try any funny stuff!" Rick gulped and stared at the man before he walked into a room next to vice-president Switzer's office. The office had two windows: one facing the rear parking lot, and another that Rick had looked into from outside. Another man with a blue shirt was sitting in a large chair behind a desk. There were several papers and file folders on the desk. The man at the desk stood up immediately. Rick realized he was a short man. The man looked up at Rick, then looked down at Rick's feet, then he looked up at him again.

"Sorry about the rough stuff, kid, but as a bank official, we have to be careful," he smiled. Rick noticed that both men wore dirty blue jeans and had about three days of stubble on their faces.

"You're a bank official? Just what do you do around here?"

"You're asking me — me, what I'm doing? No, I think you should tell us just what you were doing looking in that window. C'mon, talk!" The man in the black shirt grabbed Rick's arm again and started twisting it behind Rick's back.

"Ow! Hey, knock it off!" Rick yelled.

"All right, let him go," said the man in the blue shirt. "Hey, get his radio."

The other man tugged at Rick's radio and pulled it off his belt. He patted Rick's front and back pockets.

"I — I need that! I need it, uh, for school!"

"Oh, sure. Okay, big boy. Tell us what you're up to," said the blue-shirted man as he took the radio and put it on the desk. "We'll give you a chance to talk... oh, Ed, did you see anyone else out there?"

"Nah, just this kid... uh, I didn't really look."

"What! What were you thinking! Run outside and secure the joint. I'll keep an eye on big boy here." The man in the black shirt jogged outside. The man in the blue shirt looked down and started to talk again.

"Now's my chance... oh man!" Rick thought. He kicked the man hard in the leg and tried to grab his radio. Instead, he accidentally picked up a file folder along with the radio, but the radio fell out of his hands. Rick ran outside as fast as he could, while the man bent over howling!

"Hey!" the black-shirted man yelled when he saw Rick running. "Hold it!" But Rick ran as fast as he could toward the other parking lot where his truck was parked. He ran past a stack of plastic crates near a garbage dumpster and knocked them over.

"Aargh!" the man behind him howled. Rick turned around just quick enough to see the man tripping over the crates!

Black birds began squawking in a tree above Rick as he ran past it. The large birds flew out of the tree with a giant whoosh sound and caused a flurry of leaves to pelt Rick's face. He waved his arm violently and kept running.

Rick ran to his truck, flung open the door, and tossed down the file folder. He quickly jammed the key in the ignition and started the engine. He slammed the door shut, dropped the gearshift into gear, stomped on the accelerator and cramped the steering wheel hard to the right.

The engine stalled!

"Ah! Blast this thing!" Rick yelled. He could see the man struggling to stand up. Rick knocked the gearshift into neutral, pressed the accelerator halfway down and turned the key again. The engine roared to life. He slammed the gearshift down into gear just as Ed, the man in the black shirt, ran up to the truck. This time Rick kept the accelerator down halfway and then pressed it all the way to the floorboard.

As he drove away from the man, he saw another person step out from behind some bushes, waving his arms in front of the truck.

It was Tom!

Rick hit the brake pedal. Tom ran alongside the truck and opened the passenger door while the truck was still rolling. He jumped in and fell down on the passenger seat. He quickly sat up and slammed the door hard, just as Rick stomped his foot down on the accelerator. The exhaust system growled and barked.

They sped away from the black-shirted man, and turned sharp onto 42nd Street. The tires screeched when the truck leaned hard into the turn! After a minute, Rick noticed there were no cars behind them. He and Tom both sighed heavily.

Chapter 6

a suspicious folder

Worried that someone might follow them, Rick left the freeway a mile before the exit to the Spencer's house. He slowed down for a traffic light and rolled to a stop.

Both boys looked behind them. Another car rolled to a stop. Several other cars were stopped at the light. Behind them, a woman talked on her cell phone. An older man adjusted his radio in the car next to Tom and Rick. He looked up. The boys looked away.

Finally the light changed. Rick stepped on the gas and the old truck surged forward. The engine growled loudly through first gear, then grumbled into second gear with a jolt. Rick drove the truck another half-mile and turned down a side street.

Tom looked behind him. No one followed them. The truck continued turning down side streets. At every new street, the passenger looked behind him and the driver looked up into his rearview mirror. The truck eventually turned down the Spencer's street and rolled into the Spencer family driveway. Both boys got out of the truck and ran into the house.

Mrs. Spencer sat in the living room and looked up from her newspaper. "My goodness!" she exclaimed, "what's the rush?"

"Um, nothing, Mom," Tom panted. "Is Dad here?"

"No, he went to the police station and then he will run some errands."

The excited boys suddenly looked sadly disappointed. Mrs. Spencer continued to read her paper, but both boys quietly stood next to her. She looked up again.

"Do you boys want something?"

"Oh, uh, no Mom. Not really."

"No, Mrs. Spencer. We're... uh, we're just resting here."

"You're resting standing up?"

"Uh... yeah. Where are you going?" The boys' eyes were wide as saucers as Mrs. Spencer got out of her chair.

"I need to run upstairs for a minute." She looked at the boys. Rick cracked his knuckles for the fourth time, and Tom kept rubbing his chin and tapping his foot. "I don't know what spooked you boys, but we can talk about it if you want." She looked at Tom. "Then we can call your father."

The boys watched her walk up the stairs. Rick poked Tom with his elbow.

"How'd she know something's up?" he whispered.

"Beats me. Moms are good that way."

A few minutes later Mrs. Spencer came downstairs. She joined Tom and Rick in the living room. Mrs. Spencer sipped her tea from a dainty ceramic cup. Rick gulped water from a plastic cup and Tom drank slowly from the same kind of cup.

"Now, you drove to the bank and saw two men there, as you were saying," Mrs. Spencer said. "Then what happened?"

Rick looked at Tom. Tom looked down at the floor for a moment.

"Um... Mom, we don't want to worry you or anything... but they took Rick inside."

"And?"

"And they kept me in there!" Rick exclaimed. "I tried to get away but that guy grabbed my arm and hauled me inside. But I got away and then we drove over here. I made sure no one tailed us. But they took my radio. Man, that thing cost 40 bucks!"

Mrs. Spencer sighed. "Let's tell your father about this. Do you remember what they look like?"

"Yeah, I'll never forget 'em!" Rick answered loudly.

Mrs. Spencer telephoned her husband and told him about the bank episode. She gave the phone to Tom and he explained the details to his father. Tom reached the point in the story of jumping into the truck with Rick.

"Oh, the folder!" Rick cried. "I forgot all about it!"

"Folder?" Tom asked. "Hang on, Dad," he said into the phone.

"I accidentally grabbed a file folder from the short guy's desk before I ran out of there," Rick said. "I tried to get my radio back but I scooped up that folder instead. It's still in the truck. I'll go get it."

Tom told his father about the folder and Mr. Spencer agreed to come home with a police detective.

About an hour later Tom, Rick, Mr. and Mrs. Spencer, and Sergeant Manning from the Creekwater Police Department sat around the coffee table in the Spencer's living room. The opened file folder was on the table.

"Hmm," Sergeant Manning said.

"Mmhmm," Mr. Spencer added.

Everyone else was quiet.

"It… it just looks like a bunch of car information to me," Rick finally mumbled.

"Rick, the format of this paper is called a 'spreadsheet.' Take a closer look at these columns," Mr. Spencer said. "Tom, pay attention, too. Banks loan money so people can buy cars, right?"

"Right," both boys answered.

"If the bank is only interested in the *whole* car, then why is this column here?" Mr. Spencer pointed to a column on the spreadsheet that listed vehicle parts.

"And here's an interesting one," Sergeant Manning added. "They have prices in the next column."

Tom gasped. "Could they be taking these cars apart and selling the parts?"

"Could be," Mr. Spencer answered.

"It will be very interesting to see what turns up when we enter these cars into the police department's stolen car database," Sergeant Manning said.

Rick's eyes widened and a smile slowly formed across his face. "Aahhh!" he exclaimed.

"Rick, it's a good thing you accidentally picked up that folder!" Mrs. Spencer said. "But I don't want you boys going to that bank again. This is too dangerous now."

"Oh, Mom!" Tom cried. Mrs. Spencer held up her hand.

"It's too dangerous."

"But Mom, we'll be real careful…"

"Hold on, Thomas," Mr. Spencer interrupted. Then he turned to Sergeant Manning. "I want to see if we can get Father Spencer involved a bit more. Summers are good for him because the parish school is out." Mr. Spencer took a long breath and turned toward Tom.

"Your mother is right, and I'm certainly not going to contradict her whether you are 18 or not. But maybe you can still go there with Uncle Paul."

"Yeah," agreed Rick, "and I want my radio back."

"Oh, I'm afraid there isn't much chance of that, son," Sergeant Manning said. Rick groaned.

Mrs. Spencer didn't say anything for a moment. Then she nodded her head. "I suppose that would be all right, but I still don't want you going there without Uncle Paul or your father or a policeman."

Both boys grinned. "Okay!"

Sergeant Manning closed the folder on the coffee table and cleared his throat. "We can enter this information into the stolen car database, but it may be hard using it in court. We never had a search warrant. I'll have to find out about that."

The boys groaned, but Mr. Spencer spoke up. "Actually, the concept isn't a bad thing, although in this case it might work against us. Authorities have to have a good reason and get a search warrant from a judge instead of simply walking into a house or business and looking into things whenever they want. This civil liberty is part of our common heritage of Anglo-Saxon jurisprudence."

Both boys had blank looks on their faces.

"Huh?"

"It — it — it's part of what?"

Sergeant Manning laughed out loud. "What your father means is that we can't just take things. That's not right. We have to get permission."

"Yes, that's exactly it," added Mr. Spencer. "A search warrant is a piece of paper that gives permission to look for evidence if someone is suspected of breaking the law."

"Oh, okay. Now I get it." Both boys nodded.

"Well, Sergeant," said Mr. Spencer, "I would like to scan the spreadsheet for my records before you take it to the station, if you think that's okay." Sergeant Manning quickly agreed, and Mr. Spencer took the folder upstairs. He walked into his office and placed the first page on the glass surface of his scanner. He pushed a button on the scanner and a new window instantly appeared on his computer screen. Soon the spreadsheet appeared on the screen, and Mr. Spencer saved the image in his computer files. Then he scanned the second page. He walked downstairs, where Sergeant Manning was showing his baton and handcuffs to two eager teenage boys.

"Okay, I'm all set!" Mr. Spencer said. "Looks like you're a little busy there training some rookies," he said with a smile.

"This stuff is cool!" Tom said. "Yeah!" Rick added.

The next day, after Sunday morning Mass ended, Tom, Rick, Mr. Spencer, and Father Spencer sat around a table in St. Anne's parish office conference room. They filled Father Spencer in on the details.

"Hmm, I see what you mean," Father Spencer said to Mr. Spencer. "This case has taken an interesting turn."

"Yes," Mr. Spencer said to his brother. "And it's very important that the boys go back inside the bank to see if those men who were there Saturday are working there."

"And you need me there, too," the priest replied. The other three looked at him eagerly. "Well, of course I'll help you again!" Father Spencer agreed. "Should we pay the bank a visit tomorrow morning?"

"All right!" Both boys gave a thumbs-up.

The next morning, Tom got his car back from the shop. He smiled when he saw the seat with the new covering. Tom, Rick, and Father Spencer drove to the bank. They discussed their strategy on the way there.

"When we get there, boys," Father Spencer cautioned, "don't jump right into the office where you were held Saturday. Let's look at all the rooms first."

"Right, Uncle Paul."

"Sure thing, Father."

"Remember, this is looking more and more like an inside job. We need to keep cool and pay attention."

When they arrived at the bank, David Switzer was already in front of the main door and hurried them past the rows of busy tellers and customers into his office.

"The bank president is out," Switzer explained. "Tell me, have you found anything new?"

"The president is out again, huh?" Rick said slowly.

"Yes." Switzer said. He didn't say anything while he looked at Rick. Finally he spoke.

"Anything the matter, son?"

"I... I guess not."

"Mr. Switzer," Father Spencer said, "we would like to, ah, if you don't mind, we would like to take a look around the bank again. I can assure you we won't be in anyone's way and we don't need to talk to anyone this time. But as you know, the police are asking for our help in this case, and we need to look in each room in the bank."

"Of course, that will be fine," Switzer replied. "We need to investigate and close this case."

"We'll close the case when we catch the bank robbers," Tom said with a smile.

"Yes. Well," Switzer said, frowning, "I ah, I think we should proceed. What exactly are you looking for?" Tom started to answer but his uncle interrupted him.

"Nothing in particular," Father Spencer quickly replied. "We just need to help the police tie up some loose ends."

The priest looked at the files and papers on Switzer's desk. He stared at the stack of payroll sheets on the edge of the desk. Finally he stood up and thanked Switzer.

"Uh, Mr. Switzer," Tom said, "can you tell us who works here on Saturdays?"

"Why, no one works here on Saturdays. Why do you ask?"

"Just a thought, that's all," Tom answered. "One of our contacts thought he saw some people in the bank Saturday."

"Hmm. Oh, it could have been the cleaning crew," Switzer said with a smile. Tom and Rick frowned.

"Well, boys," Father Spencer said, "shall we start looking?" The priest turned toward Switzer. "We would like to begin in the vault."

Switzer stood up and walked outside his office. Father Spencer and the two teens followed him. They slowly walked toward the other side of the bank. Rick turned his head and looked in the office next to Switzer's, where the two men had held him. Switzer punched some numbers into a keypad on the vault door, and then turned the door handle. He held the door open for the three amateur sleuths and waved his hand.

"Much obliged," Tom said.

The three sleuths walked into the vault. Two women were sitting in front of a desk counting dollar bills. Tom looked up. There was new drywall and plaster patched into the ceiling where the robbers broke in. Rows and rows of locked metal safe-deposit boxes lined the walls. Father Spencer looked at the safe-deposit boxes and rubbed his chin. He slowly walked out-side the vault.

A small walkway lead toward rows of cubicles. The teller windows were in front of the cubicles. There were several offices at the other side of the bank, including Switzer's and the bank president's. The priest wandered toward the cubicles. Rick and Tom followed him.

The priest and the two teens looked into each cubicle. There was usually a woman or man sitting in front of a computer. Most of the bank employees in the cubicles were talking on the telephone. The three slowly walked past Bob Taylor's office, the angry loan officer. Taylor glared at the teens. Tom and Rick were secretly glad that Father Spencer was there with them. They slowly walked past all the cubicles. Father Spencer stopped in one of the cubicles and quickly waved to the person inside, who was talking on the telephone. The priest picked up two chrome valve-stem caps that were lying on a desk. He squinted his eyes.

"Can you please hold for a moment?" the bank worker said into the telephone. He looked at Father Spencer's hands, then quickly looked up at the priest.

"Can I help you with something?"

"Oh, no, not at all," the priest replied casually. "We are help-ing Mr. Switzer. I am Father Paul Spencer. And you are?"

"George Conrad," the bank worker replied with a smile. Conrad looked down at the valve-stem caps in the priest's hands again.

"Those are for my kid's bike."

"I see." The priest-investigator put the caps down. "Well, thank you for your time."

The three walked to the teller windows. They saw three bank tellers, including Christine Travinski. The priest looked at all the counters where each teller worked, but he didn't touch anything. He walked back toward the offices. Rick started to crack his knuckles and tried hard not to walk faster than the priest. Tom quickly looked behind him, but no one was looking up at them. They walked into the first office. A nameplate on the door read "Martin Sabatino, Finance Manager."

"Hello gentlemen!" Sabatino said loudly. "I saw you in David's office but I was on the phone so I couldn't say hello earlier. Helping crack the robbery, eh?"

Father Spencer smiled. "We are certainly trying."

"We haven't found anything big yet," Tom added.

They spoke for a few more minutes. The sleuths learned that Sabatino is in charge of all the loan officers at the bank. He has worked at the bank for five years. There were several folders on his desk and stacks of papers with dollar amounts and the names of several businesses. The sleuths thanked Sabatino and walked past the office next to Switzer's. They went to the bank president's office. Father Spencer tried the door but it was locked. Rick took a deep breath and walked into Switzer's office.

"The president's office is locked," Rick stated matter-of-factly.

"Oh, let me unlock it for you," Switzer answered. He stood up and followed Rick. Switzer quickly unlocked the door.

"Like I said earlier, our bank president, Mr. Reed, is away," Switzer said while he put his keys in his pants pocket. "I have to ask you please not to disturb anything in his office."

"We'll just look around," Father Spencer replied. They entered the large office. There were three windows with the shades drawn. A bookshelf and credenza were against one wall, and a couple of file cabinets against another. A large executive desk was in the rear of the office, and another smaller desk with a computer sat next to it. Switzer stood in the doorway. Father Spencer walked to the executive desk and looked at the papers on it, but didn't touch anything. Suddenly, he looked up.

"Thank you for your help," he said to Switzer. "Oh, we still have to look at that other office next to yours. Whose is it?"

Father Spencer was talking about the office that Rick was in Saturday!

"Oh, that office is empty," Switzer answered coolly. "We had an accounting manager a few months ago, but no one has been in there since. We haven't had enough people working here lately." Rick cracked his knuckles and rubbed his fingers together. His hands were sweaty. Tom shifted his weight from one foot to the other.

"I see," the priest said softly. He began walking toward the door. Switzer didn't move. Tom and Rick followed Father Spencer to the door. Switzer slowly moved to one side and the three amateur sleuths walked toward the last office. Father Spencer walked into the office first. Rick breathed hard when he recognized the windows in the office and the desk where the short man sat. Rick's eyes were as wide as saucers. Two days earlier, there were stacks of papers and file folders covering the desk. Today, the desk was empty.

"No one has used this office in months," boomed Switzer from behind the sleuths. The vice-president slowly walked past them and ran his finger along the top of the desk. He made a clean mark in the dust and sighed loudly.

"It's sort of a shame, really," Switzer said thoughtfully.

Rick and Tom both gasped.

There was a thick layer of dust on the desk and the chairs!

Chapter 7

catching big fish

Tom and Rick were speechless. Father Spencer finally cleared his throat.

"Yes, ah, well, I suppose we should get going. Paperwork to do, you know." He turned toward Switzer. "Thank you for your time. Come along, boys."

Rick started to say something but only sighed in frustration. He and Tom walked behind the priest, while Rick kept squeezing his knuckles, trying to crack them again. The three amateur sleuths slowly got into Tom's car and drove away from the bank.

"Okay, boys," Father Spencer said while they drove, "Rick, are you sure that empty office was the office you were in Saturday?"

"Absolutely!"

The priest sighed loudly. "Then something really fishy is going on at that bank," he concluded. "Tom, we need to talk to your father. He may have an idea that will help give us more clues, so we need to check with him and the police."

"Sounds good to me!" Tom replied. Rick smiled and nodded.

Later that evening, the priest joined the Spencer family for dinner. The family discussed different ways to bake chicken, the hot weather, the bank robbery case, and Tom's sister's recent visit to her grandmother's house.

"So you got back this afternoon, eh Michelle?" Father Spencer said with a smile. "How is your grandmother doing?"

"Oh, she gets tired really easy, Uncle Paul," Michelle answered. "But she still likes to do a lot of things. You should see her vegetable garden!"

"Sounds very nice," the priest said. "I'm afraid I'm not much of a gardener but I could dig a pretty big hole in my day!"

The Spencer children chuckled.

"Hopefully Michelle learned a few things from Mom," Mrs. Spencer said to Mr. Spencer. He nodded and took a sip of water from his dinner glass.

"Hey, can I have the... I mean, uh, please pass the carrots," Billy said. Mrs. Spencer looked up and smiled. Michelle handed him the bowl of steamed carrots.

"Well, John," Father Spencer said to Mr. Spencer, "as you mentioned earlier, we need to clear the plan with Creekwater police. I wonder if we could talk with Chief Roswell tomorrow?"

"I'll call him tomorrow from my office," Mr. Spencer answered. "I have a morning meeting but hopefully we could meet for lunch."

Mr. Spencer further explained his idea that evening to Tom and Father Spencer.

"It looks like an inside job," Mr. Spencer explained, "so someone needs to set a trap at the bank. We can say we are looking for evidence somewhere in town. Then, the police can watch that area to see who goes there and tries to destroy the evidence."

The next day, Chief Roswell sat in his office with the priest and Mr. Spencer. The chief filled them in on the latest developments in the case. Every car listed in the bank's spreadsheet was reported stolen within the last nine months!

While they talked, the chief quickly agreed to Mr. Spencer's plan.

"Since the security guard saw the getaway car," Mr. Spencer said, "I can telephone Switzer and tell him that your department is getting ready to look for evidence from the bank robbery at the office across the street from the bank. We'll see if anyone snoops around there to look for the evidence before the police find it."

"Hmm," Chief Roswell mumbled thoughtfully. He looked down at a stapler on his desk. "That could work."

"Well," continued Mr. Spencer with a grin, "I know your men will look at that office to see what the security guard saw. I can tell Switzer a part of your plans, and then we'll see what he does with that knowledge!"

"Ah," answered the chief with a smile. He pushed on the stapler with two fingers and looked up at the priest, then at Mr. Spencer. "Yes, we are getting ready to start looking for evidence in the parking lot at the Neighborly Insurance Agency, so you can tell him that."

"I'll talk to Holmes," Father Spencer said, "and ask him to help watch for anything."

"That's fine, Father," the police chief answered. "We could have Holmes leave his post for a few nights to make it easier for the robbers to come back. But I think that would make it too easy and the robbers might get suspicious of the trap." Chief Roswell picked up the stapler and squeezed it. A spent staple fell out and landed on his desk.

"Yes," Mr. Spencer agreed immediately, "that's a very good point. Oh, do you want me to inform the agency manager there and assure the office staff that they will be protected?"

"Yes, go ahead," Chief Roswell answered. "That would help our police department get some other work done on this case."

The next day, Chief Roswell told Mr. Spencer everything was set and he could make his phone call. The detective took a deep breath and prayed a *Hail Mary*, then picked up his phone and dialed. He heard the phone ring once, then a woman's voice.

"Creekwater National Bank, may I help you?"

"Yes, David Switzer, please. This is John Spencer."

"One moment..." Mr. Spencer could hear the phone ring again.

"This is David."

"Mr. Switzer! This is John Spencer..."

"Ah, Mr. Spencer! How are you doing?"

"Oh, very well, thank you! Actually, I have good news for you."

"Oh?"

"Yes, it turns out the police found some hard evidence from the bank robbery! I wanted to let you know about it."

"Really! What did they find?"

"Well, they didn't tell me very much. They said they found the getaway car and some evidence in it."

"I see. Did they tell you anything else?"

"Oh, yes. They are getting ready to look for evidence at the Neighborly Insurance Agency right across the street from your bank! Something about the parking lot there. But that's all they told me."

"Well, that is interesting, John. Thank you so much for letting me know," Switzer said.

"Well, like I said, I wanted to keep you informed if we found anything."

"Did you need anything else from me? Oh, how are those boys doing?"

"Ah, no, nothing else. And my son and his friend are just fine. They're both starting college in the fall, you know. I need to run, but I'll talk to you later."

"Okay. Thank you again for calling."

"You're quite welcome. Goodbye for now."

"Goodbye."

Mr. Spencer slowly hung up the phone and sighed deeply. He leaned back in his chair and looked at a small statue of Saint Joseph on his desk.

"We'll see if that traps any bait, eh?" he thought to himself.

Meanwhile, Rick Kline slept in late that morning. It was already warm outside by the time he started the yard work in his backyard.

"Man, it's hot out here!" Rick thought to himself. He tossed a trash bag of leaves and grass clippings into a big garbage can behind the Kline house and walked inside. He refilled his water glass and sat down. His mother looked at him.

"Well, when you were little," Mrs. Kline said, "and everyone called you Ricky, I woke you up on time. But now it's up to you."

Rick sighed loudly. "Yeah, well," he panted. "I'll be done soon!"

"After your shower, I want you to work on those scholarship applications again. We have…"

"Oh, Mom, I was going to help Tom!"

"Don't interrupt me. We have to get those in before the spring deadline."

Rick sighed. "I know, and I was gonna work on 'em later. I need to go help Tom."

Mrs. Kline looked at her son. She didn't say anything for almost a whole minute. Finally, she took a long breath.

"I know the Spencers are good people," she said slowly in a terse, firm voice. "But all this detective work makes me nervous. I know you're 18 now but you have to get those applications done tonight."

Rick didn't say anything. He quickly got up from his chair and went back outside.

The next day, Rick and Tom spent the afternoon with two police officers on a "surveillance" job watching the Neighborly Insurance Agency. They were sitting in a parked van in the parking lot next to the insurance agency's parking lot. The van had a sliding panel that separated the two front seats from the rear of the van. The van had a television monitor, a computer, a hidden antenna, a two-way radio, a rifle rack with two rifles and some boxes of ammunition, two binoculars, and a small wooden desktop near the back seat. The television monitor picked up images inside the insurance agency from a hidden police camera. The outside of the van had a sign on each side that read "Helen's Flowers."

That evening Rick stayed at the Spencer house. After dinner, Tom and Rick talked to Mr. Spencer in his den.

"We didn't see anything today, Dad," Tom said.

"Yeah, but all that police equipment sure is cool!" Rick added. "They sure have more stuff than Tom and I do."

Mr. Spencer laughed. "Well, it sounds like you two probably learned a lot." He pulled a file folder out of his briefcase. "I have news for you," he said. Tom and Rick leaned forward in their chairs as Mr. Spencer thumbed through his folder. He began speaking again in a low voice, without looking up. "I found the owners of that burned getaway car today. Let's see, it's in here somewhere…" Rick and Tom gasped.

"You — Dad, you found the owners!"

"Mr. Spencer, did the police arrest them?"

Mr. Spencer looked up. "Oh, no, not at all," he replied. "The car was stolen and the owners are completely innocent. Victims, actually. Ah, here's the paperwork. Mr. and Mrs. Lockwood. They live in Pricklypatch. Nice elderly couple. Their insurance company already settled with them."

"Pricklypatch. That's a ways from here," Rick said.

"Ah! Maybe they were the ones who changed that tire," exclaimed Tom, "since Pricklypatch is out in the country!"

"Bingo," replied Mr. Spencer. "Mr. Lockwood confirmed it. He changed the tire before it was stolen. Since the car was burned, I had to cross-reference the make and model from the police and insurance records because we didn't have the Vehicle Identification Number."

"Did Chief Roswell's people find out if all those cars in the spreadsheet were stolen too?" Tom asked thoughtfully.

"Yes, that's exactly what they found," Mr. Spencer answered. He looked at Rick. "Actually, Rick, I wanted to talk to you about that." The elder Spencer looked down at his file folder again. Rick sat up in his chair and cleared his throat. Mr. Spencer finished looking at the folder and looked up at Rick again. "When they held you inside the bank, do you remember any other papers on that desk?"

"Yeah! There was a bunch. The whole desk was covered with papers and file folders and there were a couple lug nuts, too."

"Lug nuts?" Tom asked.

"Yeah. I forgot until now," Rick answered. "You know, those nuts that hold a wheel onto a car. There were three or four chrome ones on the desk."

"Hmm," Mr. Spencer said. He squinted his eyes and tapped his fingers on his desk.

"Did Uncle Paul tell you about those valve-stem caps he saw in someone's cubicle, Dad?" Tom asked.

"Yes, he did." Mr. Spencer looked up at the ceiling and kept tapping his fingers on his desk. Finally, he spoke up again. "Do you remember seeing any other car parts?"

Rick sighed. "Nope. Nothing else."

"Hmm."

Tom sat up in his chair. "Dad," he asked, "are you thinking what I'm thinking?"

"I'm thinking what you're thinking, I think," Mr. Spencer answered with a grin.

"I think we're on to something here," Tom said, "if you think you're thinking what I'm thinking, I think."

"Oh, stop!" Rick laughed. "What's going on?"

"A stolen car ring, son," Mr. Spencer said.

"And somehow, people at the bank are mixed up in it," Tom added. "But how?"

"That's what we — and Chief Roswell's men — have to find out!" Mr. Spencer said.

The next morning, Rick drove to the Spencer house in his father's old pickup truck. When he pulled up to the driveway, Michelle and Tom walked outside. There were a few big billowy clouds breaking up the vast blue sky over the Creekwater suburbs.

"Hey, man," Tom said as he walked up to Rick. "That's a pretty handy truck. You didn't even have to ring our doorbell, because all the windows in the house started shaking when you got here."

"Yeah, yeah, wise guy," Rick answered with a smile. He got out of the truck. Michelle looked up at him and smiled.

"Hi, Rick," she said slowly in a sing-song voice.

"Hey, Michelle," Rick said with a smile. "How are you? Wait, don't answer that. Lemme guess, you're doing fine?" Michelle giggled. "So what's new? So what's old?" Rick asked. Michelle giggled louder.

"Well you two," Tom said, "sorry to break this up, but we have to get to the police station."

"Oh yeah, huh," Rick suddenly grunted. Michelle said good-bye while Tom and Rick walked to the garage and climbed into Tom's Mustang. A second later the car's engine roared awake and the twin chrome exhaust pipes barked rudely at the Spencer house as the two boys pulled out of the driveway.

The boys arrived at the police station and talked with Officers Meyer and Wilson. The four of them drove in the surveillance van. They returned to the parking lot next to the Neighborly Insurance Agency. They sat there more than two hours watching people coming and going. Every hour, one of the officers would radio in to the station.

Every police vehicle has a number assigned to it. The van's number is 6B3. When using the radio, the officers say that their van number 6B3 is "Six Baker Three." They also reported the name of the case they are working on. This case is named "Operation Big Fish."

"Six Baker Three, Operation Big Fish. No activity."

"Roger, Six Baker Three," a female voice responded.

They sat another hour. A few cars and trucks drove in and out of the parking lot. People walked in and out of the insurance agency and the other offices in the building. Officer Wilson picked up the radio microphone and pushed a button on the side of it.

"Six Baker Three, Operation Big Fish. No activity," he said into the microphone.

"Roger, Six Baker Three," came the reply.

A few minutes later, a pickup truck with two men pulled into the parking lot and a man climbed out of the passenger seat. He walked into the agency. When he walked back to the truck, a small dog darted out of the truck and ran away. The man ran after the dog and waved to the truck. The man in the truck drove slowly toward the dog. Then the truck turned slowly and drove the other direction. The man in the parking lot kept walking around, looking for the dog.

"Hey, look at this," Officer Meyer said. Officer Wilson picked up his binoculars and looked at the man in the parking lot.

"He's looking all over the lot," Wilson said. "Did he lose his dog, or...what? Hmm."

Tom and Rick shifted excitedly in their seats. They tried to peek out the back windows of the van. The pickup truck drove slowly to the other side of the parking lot. The man in the parking lot began looking under the bushes lining the parking lot. Officer Meyer handed Rick a pair of binoculars.

"Here you go, son," Meyer said. "Take a look." Rick looked through the binoculars. He gasped!

"Tom!" Rick cried. "That's the tall guy who grabbed me by the arm and held me inside the bank!"

"That guy looking under the bushes?" Tom asked nervously.

"Yeah!"

"Rick," asked Officer Meyer, "can you positively identify that man? Are you sure?"

"Yeah! No doubt!"

"Six Baker Three," Meyer said into the microphone. "Operation Big Fish caught bait."

"Roger, Six Baker Three," came the reply.

"Six Baker Three, two leads. Both Caucasian male. No distinguishing marks. Continuing to monitor," Meyer added.

"Copy, Six Baker Three. Awaiting instructions."

"Copy."

Officer Wilson put down his binoculars. He reached over to the rifle rack and picked up a brown rifle with a magnifying scope on top of it. Rick looked at him, then looked at the man near the bushes.

"Do you think he has a gun?" Rick asked Officer Wilson.

"I don't know. But in situations like this we need to stay prepared, so I'm getting the rifle ready just in case."

"May I use the binoculars?" Tom asked.

"Sure, go ahead," Wilson answered. He jerked the bolt on the rifle and it snapped loudly into place. Tom picked up the binoculars and held them up to his face. He adjusted the lenses and looked at the man near the bushes. Then he looked across the parking lot at the other man driving the truck.

"Hey, it's that Conrad guy!" Tom yelled. "Officer Wilson, the man driving the truck works at the bank. My uncle saw him with some valve-stem caps."

"Are you sure?"

"Yes. His last name is Conrad. Uncle Paul — Father Paul Spencer — talked to him at the bank a few days ago. I was with him."

"Six Baker Three," Officer Meyer said into the microphone.

"Copy, Six Baker Three," said the female voice over the radio's speaker.

"Lead Two positively identified. Name is Conrad, works at the bank. No name for Lead One."

"Copy, Six Baker Three," the voice from the radio said.

"Hey, wait, I remember!" Rick cried. "That tall guy's name is Ed. That's what the other guy in the bank called him when they held me there."

"Six Baker Three, Lead One apparently goes by first name of Ed."

"Copy, Six Baker Three."

The man looking under the bushes stood up straight. He looked around, then began walking toward the insurance agency's front door. The man in the pickup truck drove behind the building where the officers in the van couldn't see him.

"Six Baker Three," Meyer said into the microphone. "Request backup. Code blue. Lead One walking into the insurance agency again."

"Copy, Six Baker Three," the female voice said. "All units near 42nd Street and Broadway. Operation Big Fish needs backup. Code Blue."

"Seven Adam Six, copy that, dispatch," a male voice said from the radio. "ETA two minutes."

Officer Wilson held the butt of his rifle between his chest and right shoulder, aimed the barrel toward the front door of the insurance agency, and waited.

Chapter 8

....

the meeting

The backup police car arrived quietly and pulled into the same parking lot as the surveillance van. The car's emergency lights were off. Officer Meyer spoke into the radio microphone.

"Six Baker Three, Seven Adam Six, still code blue, cover not blown. Suspects positively identified. One driving mid '90s F150 pickup behind offices. Can you see him?"

"Roger, Six Baker Three," a male voice said over the radio. "F150 driving slowly behind office... he's coming around the building now. I'll stay back here... I don't think he can see the car."

"Roger. We lost sight of the truck. We have line of sight on other suspect." Ed, the man who walked toward the front of the insurance agency, stopped and looked around the front door of the agency. He walked up and down the front sidewalk of the office.

"Ah," Officer Meyer said, "here comes the truck again." The pickup truck slowly drove around the other side of the building. Ed walked toward the truck. Officer Wilson lowered his rifle and watched. Ed said something to Conrad, the driver of the truck. Then Ed walked around the truck. Suddenly the dog ran out from some bushes and jumped into the truck. Ed climbed in, and the truck turned toward the street. Tom watched them through the police binoculars and Rick squinted his eyes to see the truck clearly.

"Seven Adam Six, Six Baker Three," the officer in the squad car said over the radio. "Please advise... do we pursue?"

"Negative," Meyer said into the microphone. "We need an unmarked unit for surveillance. They probably saw this van already as well." Meyer nodded to Wilson, who put his rifle away and jumped into the driver's seat. He started driving. He wanted to follow the truck at a safe distance so they wouldn't be noticed.

Officer Meyer clicked the button on the radio microphone again. "Six Baker Three to dispatch."

"Copy, Six Baker Three," a female voice said over the radio.

"Request unmarked surveillance pursuit, white mid-'90s Ford F150 regular cab. Leaving Neighborly Insurance Agency at 42nd and Broadway... heading west on Broadway... following at a distance."

"Copy. Unit Two Baker Ten is already dispatched."

"Two Baker Ten? That's Manning's car," Wilson said to Meyer. "He must be taking a real interest in this case."

"Roger, dispatch," Officer Meyer said into the radio microphone. Then he cleared his throat. "Six Baker Three, Seven Adam Six, can you follow about 100 yards behind us?"

"Roger that!" said the officer in the squad car.

"Um, Officer Meyer?" Tom asked.

"Huh? Oh, yes?"

"When that guy Ed walked around the truck, I saw him purse his lips, like he was whistling. That was right before that dog came out of nowhere."

Officers Wilson and Meyer looked at each other.

"These guys try real hard," Wilson laughed. "But they're not too smart."

Officer Meyer patted Tom on the shoulder. "Good detective work, son."

Suddenly another male voice boomed over the radio. "Two Baker Ten, Six Baker Three. Suspect in sight. I'm three cars behind you. Let me take 'em."

"Roger, Sergeant," Officer Meyer answered into the microphone. Wilson turned right down the next street. Meanwhile, the two cars that were behind the officers' van drove straight and a new blue Ford LTD sedan passed them both, until it was directly behind the Ford truck.

"Two Baker Ten," the four investigators heard Sergeant Manning say from the radio.

"Copy, Two Baker Ten," a female voice answered.

"Surveillance pursuit of F150, license two-Baker-John-four-nine-seven. They are turning into the bank," Sergeant Manning said.

"Copy, Two Baker Ten," the female voice responded.

The whole time Conrad drove the truck, he only went around a square mile and came back to the bank, across the street from Neighborly Insurance Agency!

Officer Wilson drove the van back to police headquarters. While they drove, Tom and Rick kept listening to the radio. There was silence for a few minutes. The dispatcher reported a traffic accident at Elm and 32nd Street. Another officer said he was on his way. There was another minute of silence. Sergeant Manning's voice came across the radio again.

"Two Baker Ten."

"Copy, Two Baker Ten," the female voice answered.

"Truck driver entered bank. Passenger now driving alone, heading south on 42nd Street."

"Copy, Two Baker Ten."

"That's Conrad, right Tom?" Officer Meyer asked. "Conrad was the guy driving the truck, and now he went into the bank?"

"Yes, that's right," Tom replied. "So now Ed is driving, uh, south on 42nd Street."

"I hope they catch that guy!" Rick exclaimed.

Tom and Rick later learned that Ed drove to some worn-down townhouses on the south side of town.

That afternoon, they discussed their day with Tom's father in his den.

"Can you believe that, Mr. Spencer?" Rick asked. "Man, we got those guys for sure now!"

"We certainly do. But do we have *all* of them? We still haven't uncovered that whole car theft ring, and we have no idea where the stolen bank money is — or which one of them stole it," Mr. Spencer replied.

"Yeah, that's true," Rick said sadly.

"Oh, don't worry too much about that," Tom said excitedly. "We'll catch them all, huh Dad?"

"We're definitely on our way," Mr. Spencer said with a smile. "I talked with Chief Roswell and Sergeant Manning before I came home today. They traced the truck plates to those townhouses and the truck is registered to an address there."

"You mean we know where Ed lives?" Rick gasped.

"He drove home when Sergeant Manning followed him?" Tom asked.

"Yes," Mr. Spencer answered. "Let's see..." he began clicking the mouse on his computer, then he pressed a key on the keyboard. "Edward Miller, 1202 East Palmview Drive, Creekwater. Twelfth and Palmview, not a very nice area."

"I don't think we want to look around there," Tom said.

"Speak for yourself," Rick retorted. "We need to catch all these guys!"

"Hold on, boys," Mr. Spencer said. "We still have some old-fashioned, simple detective work to do. How about we go over every car on that spreadsheet and find their addresses?"

The boys frowned. "Oh yeah," Tom said.

"Humpf, yeah," Rick grunted.

"Relax," Mr. Spencer said. "You'll have plenty of more 'exciting' things to do later. Remember detective work can be very complicated! You have to pay attention to details. That's what Father Spencer is so good at."

Over the next several days, the boys researched the vehicle information on the spreadsheet and checked it against the

Department of Motor Vehicle records. They discovered that every car on the spreadsheet was registered to an address somewhere between the east side of town and Pricklypatch.

"Creekwater National Bank is on the east side of town!" Tom exclaimed.

"And the burned getaway car is from Pricklypatch!" Rick added.

"Well," Tom said thoughtfully, "we know where these people operate. That narrows it down."

That evening, the Spencer family sat down to dinner together with Rick as their guest. Rick happily sat next to Michelle when it looked like there happened to be an empty chair next to her. Actually, Michelle spent all day helping her mother plan the dinner and she loudly argued with the younger Spencer boys, Billy and Jason, about where to put the extra chair.

"Dad, how is the case going down at police headquarters?" Tom asked after sipping his water.

"At this point," Mr. Spencer said between bites of pot roast, "Roswell is talking with the DA about the bank robbery."

"What's the Dee-A?" Jason asked.

"That's the district attorney," Tom quickly answered. "He's the one who helps make sure bad guys go to jail."

"Please pass the roast beef."

"There you go."

"Thanks."

"So," Rick said after swallowing hard, "the DA is building a case against that Ed Miller guy and Conrad at the bank? That's great." Michelle looked up at Rick and smiled while he spoke.

"Oh, it's much more than that," Mr. Spencer replied. "We are uncovering a hornet's nest, as it were. Roswell's men can't go in yet and arrest them because they want to catch everyone involved in the bank robbery and the stolen car ring, too."

"Please pass the carrots... thanks."

"Mom, can I — may I have some more please?"

"Sure, honey. More pot roast?"

"Yeah." Mrs. Spencer cut some more roast for Jason.

"Wonder where all those stolen cars are," Rick said.

"That's a good question," Tom added.

Mr. Spencer looked up from his dinner plate. "Hopefully we'll find out."

The next day Chief Roswell held a general meeting in a conference room at police headquarters. Besides the chief, the others attending the meeting were Mr. Spencer, Tom, Rick, Father Spencer, Sergeant Manning, Officer Meyer, another officer the boys hadn't met yet, and two dozen doughnuts.

The chief introduced everyone to Tom, Rick, and Father Spencer. The chief then introduced Officer Spiegel to the three amateur sleuths. Spiegel is assisting Sergeant Manning.

"I really appreciate you bringing us into your meeting, Chief Roswell," Tom said.

"Oh, not a problem. You and Rick are both a part of this case." Sergeant Manning opened the curtains to a window while Officer Meyer and Father Spencer both tried to grab the same doughnut. The middle-aged man of God and church apologized to the young man of law and order. Father Spencer picked up a different doughnut while Chief Roswell picked up a dry-erase marker. The chief began writing on a large white marker board hanging on the wall. He wrote the names of the top bank executives on one side of the board. He then drew a rough map on the other side of the board, showing three "X" marks: one for the bank, another for Ed Miller's townhouse, and a third for Pricklypatch. Next, the police chief put a check mark next to the executives who were suspects in the bank robbery. There was only one: David Switzer, Vice-President. Chief Roswell explained his drawing to everyone at the meeting. He then turned to Sergeant Manning.

"Sergeant, would you please fill us in on the stolen car ring?"

There was a dozen doughnuts left.

"OK... let's see..." the police sergeant stood up and walked to the front of the room. He pointed to the map. "Thanks to these two boys and their hard work, we know that every stolen car on that list was between this general area… and here." He pointed to the bank, then to Pricklypatch. "We don't have the big picture yet. We only know some of the players, like Miller, but we don't know who is running the show."

Officer Spiegel took another doughnut.

"Now, we have a few options before us," Sergeant Manning continued. "We can watch Miller for a few days and arrest him and his associates. The DA will help us with a plea bargain if Miller tells us — informs for us — who runs the crime ring. Most of you in this room know by now that you get what you pay for when you use informers. How do we know he will really tell the truth?"

Sergeant Manning put his hand to his face and continued speaking. "Another option is to wait, keep doing surveillance and research, talk to the car owners, watch that bank, and try to piece the whole thing together. The problem with that is time. The longer we wait, the harder these thieves will try to elude us." The sergeant drank from a cup of coffee.

"What's the third option?" Mr. Spencer said with a loud sigh.

Sergeant Manning finished his coffee. "The third option… the third option is to focus our efforts — concentrate our resources on finding those cars, or at least the parts. This is an active car ring we are talking about. We know they had something to do with the bank robbery because the same people are involved. So the third option includes a theory: find the cars, and you will find the stolen money, too."

"I like that idea," Officer Meyer said.

While Sergeant Manning continued to talk, Rick whispered to Officer Spiegel. "How come they can't do everything in option two, like watch the bank and talk to the car owners and stuff, and also work on finding the cars?"

Spiegel leaned over and answered Rick quietly. "We don't have the money or enough manpower to do all that at once. We have to do one or the other for right now, and we'll get more help from a state or federal police agency a little later. That's usually how these things work."

There were seven doughnuts left. Chief Roswell looked at some papers in his left hand while he twirled a crooked paper clip around his right fingers. Finally he spoke up.

"We still need to find out if these car parts are going out of state or out of the country," the chief said. "If either one is the case, then we will get help from the FBI."

"Well, we need to jump on this car ring then, so we can see if we can get outside help as quickly as possible," Officer Meyer concluded.

"We know about some of these car parts, but all we've seen so far are lug nuts and valve-stem caps," said Sergeant Manning. "We haven't tracked a single large part yet with a part number, let alone a whole car with a VIN!"

"But if we spend a week — two weekends — tailing Miller, we may find those parts," added Officer Spiegel.

Two policemen began talking at once, then Chief Roswell interrupted and brought up the idea that he will assign more people to this case if no new leads are developed in the next seven days. Someone else at the table pointed to the map and asked if they could get help from the county sheriff's office now, since Pricklypatch is involved. Suddenly, the tall, lanky middle-aged priest who was all but forgotten in the conversation interrupted all the professional lawmen.

"Payroll sheets!" blurted Father Spencer.

"What?" exclaimed the frustrated police chief. Suddenly everyone in the room was quiet and they all looked at Father Spencer. No one noticed that there were only four doughnuts left.

"Payroll sheets," the priest repeated. "Of course. That's just it! Don't you see? As you policemen like to say, it's motive, means and opportunity, isn't it? Well, there you have the motive. A man needs a motive to choose to commit evil, after all. It's a positive act of the will. No one is born evil, you know. A man must make a choice, an act of the will, to commit evil, and for that he needs a motive, or…"

"Father!" Sergeant Manning exclaimed. He held his hand to his forehead and shook his head. "What... what on earth are you talking about?"

"Why, the payroll sheets, of course," the priest answered innocently. "A man who achieves an important position as vice-president of a bank would suffer wounded pride — very wounded pride — if he had to run the employee payroll. I didn't think of it before, because of course the payroll is a very important job and most anyone would be proud to have the responsibility. But a vice-president who has other duties might not think so, don't you think?"

Sergeant Manning looked exasperated. "I... I suppose. I guess."

"What does this have to do with the car theft ring?" demanded Chief Roswell. The paper clip was completely straightened out in his hands. Someone must have noticed that there were only four doughnuts left, because now there were only three.

"Paul, what are you getting at?" asked Mr. Spencer.

"The motive, the motive!" Father Spencer rubbed his chin. "It's so simple now that I can see the thing clearly. Why would a man want to rob his own bank? He would have to be either very poor, which a vice-president is not, or very disgruntled — very upset at his employer. Would you want to take over running payroll if you were an executive? The anger at what the executive thinks is the humility of such a thing just boils inside you. It doesn't really matter what the job is, it's the pride — oh, that pride, that power. It's like a cancer, really, lying hidden until, well, ah, lying hidden until the means and the opportunity arrive. Then you act, man!"

Sergeant Manning sighed loudly. He and Chief Roswell looked at each other. "Father," the sergeant said, "we appreciate your contribution, but I think it might be a bit of a stretch."

"Wait a minute," Officer Spiegel said. "I think the priest is on to something."

"Well, Father Spencer," the police chief replied, "if you wish, you can certainly look into that idea further. Switzer is obviously involved in the bank robbery somehow, and we don't know all the details yet."

The chief stood up and looked around the room. "Gentlemen! We will do option two. We will continue researching this entire thing, we will do surveillance on the bank, we will talk to the car owners, and we will follow Mr. Miller for a week. I know time isn't on our side and the thieves may get wise to us. I think if we follow the rats, we will find their nest. So I want to use all available manpower to look into this thing from every angle. If our detective work is detailed enough, we will find those cars and the car parts anyway. Mr. Spencer, Father Spencer, boys, I want to thank all of you for coming to this meeting."

The other policemen at the table nodded their heads and walked back to their desks. Sergeant Manning gave Mr. Spencer the last three doughnuts to take home.

That afternoon, Tom and Rick discussed the meeting.

"Seems kind of a shame they aren't going to really look for the stolen cars," Rick mumbled.

"Oh, they'll still look for them," Tom answered. "But they will work on the entire case, not just finding the stolen cars."

"Yeah," Rick agreed. He sighed and didn't say anything for a few seconds. "You know, there's nothing stopping us from looking for those cars."

"By ourselves?" Tom gasped.

"Well, yeah! Why not? We should go for it."

"It's dangerous. This is really dangerous," Tom replied.

"We have our phones, we have the cops for backup, we have your dad. Come on, man, nothin'll happen to us! Let's start looking around," Rick said.

"Like nothing happened to us when we snooped around the bank that Saturday."

"Oh, yeah. Hmm." Rick didn't say anything for a few seconds. "Yeah, let's look for the cars and the parts anyway. We'll just have to watch our backs! We have to catch these guys!"

"This is too dangerous!" Tom countered.

"I want to catch those guys. Don't you want to catch them? Actually, all we have to do is find where they take the cars. We don't have to try to hold them or anything like that. They won't even know we're there. Let's leave all that paperwork and all those phone calls and all that boring stuff to the police department. You and I are going to find some stolen cars!"

Tom quietly looked down. He kicked the ground and cracked his knuckles. "All right... all right!" he said. "I don't know why I let you talk me into this, but we need to do something."

"Yeah!" Rick exclaimed. He stuck his thumb up.

Tom gave a thumbs-up, too. "Let's do it!"

Chapter 9

traveling sleuths

Tom and Rick loaded their gear into Tom's car early the next morning. Rick had a new radio he bought to replace the one that was taken at the bank. He and Tom both put their radios on the back seat. Tom also put his spy-listening kit on the back seat. The boys loaded up the trunk with their flashlights, binoculars, digital cameras, and Tom's laptop. They each had a buck knife in their pockets and cell phones clipped onto their belts.

Tom drove to a gas station and filled up his gas tank. The boys bought cold drinking water at the station. Although they both already had breakfast, they bought sweet rolls, too.

The miles flew by quickly as Tom drove out of town. Finally they cleared the last of eastern Creekwater's rows of office buildings and houses and were driving into the desert wilderness. The highway narrowed. Tom carefully kept his Mustang between the painted lines in the road as they drove into the sunrise at highway speed.

It was a great day for adventure, Rick thought. The sunrise splashed brilliant hues of red and orange onto the few wispy clouds in the eastern sky. The sky behind them still had the deep purple coating of pre-dawn darkness. As the light breaks up the darkness, Rick thought to himself, so he and Tom will break up this car theft ring. What could possibly go wrong?

Tom turned on the radio and they listened to the news and the weather report. The day will be a typical summer day in their part of the country: hot and dry.

The boys finally traveled the 60 miles from northeast Creekwater to Pricklypatch. Tom drove the Mustang into a truck stop. The boys climbed out of the car, stretched their legs, and looked around. There were several semi trucks in the parking lot, a few recreational vehicles and family cars sitting at the gas pumps, and many people walking through the front door of the store. The boys walked into the store and bought more drinking water. Tom asked the clerk if he knew anything about the stolen cars.

"I heard about that, yeah," answered the clerk. "My car wasn't stolen, not that it would be a big loss. But I hear tell around town there's been a few car thefts here."

"Do you know anyone whose car was stolen?" Tom asked.

"Nah. Why you want to know? Your car get stoled too?"

"No," Tom replied casually. "Just wondering, ah, just wondering how safe it is here."

"Oh, don't worry about that," the clerk replied as he finished ringing up their purchases. "This ain't the big city."

Tom took the receipt from the clerk. They walked away from the counter so others behind them could pay for their purchases. They walked back to the Mustang and climbed in. Tom started the engine and turned on the air conditioner. He sat still, looked out the windshield and didn't drive away.

"Thinking about the case?" Rick asked. He could tell by the look on Tom's face when he was thinking about something important.

"Where would you hide a bunch of stolen cars?" Tom asked while still looking straight ahead.

"Maybe a big warehouse."

Tom didn't say anything for a few seconds. "Maybe," he finally said softly. "If they have the cars here in Pricklypatch, which I think they do, then what if there aren't any warehouses in this small town?"

"What if they have the cars in Creekwater?" Rick asked.

"They could. But look how big Creekwater is. The police there have a whole unit just for stolen cars. Wouldn't it be a lot easier to get away with the thefts if you kept the cars in a small run-down town with hardly any cops?" Tom said.

Rick thought for a few moments. "If there's a bunch of stolen cars and the police find out, there will be a swarm of out-of-town cops coming down here! But if the cars are here, then where are they?"

Neither of them said anything for a few seconds.

"Body shop?" Tom wondered out loud. "Car repair shop?"

"Maybe a junkyard," Rick said.

"A junkyard. A junkyard!" Tom said excitedly. "That's it! There has to be a junkyard in a beat-up town like this." He put the car in gear and started driving.

They drove to another gas station a couple miles away. The station had an older-style attendant booth instead of a store. The booth had a scratched up half-open window with a small counter under it. They walked to the window and asked the clerk if she knew of any junkyards in town. The clerk told him there were two junkyards in the area, one near the highway and another smaller one on a dirt road just outside Pricklypatch. Both boys thanked her and jogged back to the car.

They drove back on the main highway past the first truck stop they visited earlier. A few minutes later Tom spotted the exit sign for the junkyard near the highway. He braked gradually. He slowly drove toward the junkyard. The boys saw a lot of older beat-up cars without wheels and a single-wide trailer. Tom parked the car a few hundred feet away from the junkyard and both boys climbed out of the car. They took off their cell phones and picked up their radios from the back seat. Tom clipped his spy-listening kit to his belt and put the headphones on while Rick got his camera from the trunk. They walked slowly toward the beat-up cars.

Tom looked at all the cars on the dirt lot. He motioned to Rick to take pictures on the far side of the lot. Tom bent over so his body was lower than the window on the side of the trailer. He slowly walked up to the trailer and knelt down next to the window. He put the spy kit's suction cup on the edge of the window and adjusted the volume knob on the listening device.

"That will work," he heard a male voice say from the listening kit. "Yes, we can tow the car, it's no problem. Glad... of service." The voice was breaking up. Tom adjusted the controls on the listening device. He heard the voice say goodbye and then he heard a click. He heard some paper shuffling.

Tom stayed there another minute, then looked around for Rick. He saw Rick walking around the other side of the trailer. Tom took off the suction cup, quickly peered inside the window, and then crept toward Rick.

"See anything?" Tom whispered.

"Yeah," Rick answered. "A bunch of beat up old wrecks. But I took pictures."

"Let's go," Tom said. Both boys crept away from the trailer until they were behind a rusted car, then they stood up straight and walked toward Tom's Mustang.

As they drove away from the junkyard, they discussed the place.

"I don't think there's anything fishy at that junkyard," Tom said. "There was a guy in the trailer talking about getting another wreck for his yard. And they are too close to the highway, don't you think?"

"That's true," Rick said. "I guess it would be pretty obvious if they had stolen cars there, right off the main highway!"

"Besides," Tom added, "I saw a cross hanging on the wall inside the trailer."

"Hmm," Rick said thoughtfully. "Maybe they just want to look like good Christians and they are dealing in a stolen-car racket! Or, well, maybe they really are good people."

"Let's check out that other junkyard," Tom suggested.

Tom drove on the highway to the Frontier Road exit, just outside Pricklypatch. Frontier is a dirt road that seemed to go through the middle of nowhere. They drove on the dirt road for two miles, passing a few trees, some large bushes, and a lot of cacti. They didn't see any buildings or signs of life nearby. They reached a little hill in the dirt road, where on the right they could see a couple buildings far off in the distance surrounded by trees. Tom concluded they must be part of a farm. They could also see the junkyard a little more than a mile ahead.

"I think we ought to drive all the way up to it," Tom said.

"Oh, man! Are you sure?"

"Yeah," Tom answered. "I want to see if they take walk-in customers or if they only deal with wholesalers. You know, like crooked businessmen who deal in stolen car parts."

"Ah, gotcha," Rick smiled. He stuck his thumb up.

"And," Tom said, "I want to get a really good look at that place, a broader view than if we were on foot." Tom stuck his thumb up, too.

Tom slowed the Mustang and turned into the junkyard's dirt lot. Immediately, two large German shepherds bounded up from the shade of a rusted car and ran toward the Mustang! Tom and Rick could see the dogs' sharp teeth as they barked wildly. Rick tried to get out of the car but both dogs put their front paws on the passenger window of the Mustang. They growled and barked at Rick's face. A heavy gruff-looking man ambled out of a trailer home and began yelling at the dogs.

"Heel! Heel!" The dogs sat down but they both snarled at Rick. Tom opened his door and one of the dogs bolted around the car, barking. The other dog stood up and began barking at Rick again. Tom slammed his door shut while Rick lowered his window.

"What do you want here?" The unshaven man demanded.

"We, uh, we are looking for Ford parts," yelled Tom over the barking dogs. "For my car!"

"Well, beat it! We don't sell retail."

"You don't sell any parts to people?" Rick shouted.

"No. We are a wholesale outfit. Now scram! You're bothering my dogs!"

Tom put the gearshift into reverse and slowly backed out of the dirt lot. Rick raised his window and they both looked around. There were dozens of old wrecks, but a few newer Hondas and Toyotas, too. Tom saw about a half-dozen newer pickup trucks behind the trailer home. He backed out to Frontier Road, put his car in gear, and slowly drove away.

"*We* were bothering his dogs?" Rick scoffed. "We bothered the dogs? I thought it was the other way around!"

"No kidding!" Tom said. "That guy sure seemed to be hiding something."

"The newest car at the other junkyard was about 15 or 20 years old," Rick noted.

Tom drove for another minute and went over the hill where they first saw the junkyard. He eased off the accelerator, then braked. He pulled over.

"What's going on?" Rick asked.

"I have an idea."

"Let's hear it!" Rick stuck his thumb up.

"The guy at the junkyard can see all the way to that hill," Tom said. "But he can't see beyond it. So we park behind the hill, and walk back."

"Walk back?!" Rick gasped. "In this heat! And what about the dogs!"

"Well," Tom smiled, "there's nothing I can do about the heat, but we have our water. For the dogs, my spy-listening kit has an ultra-sonic function." He pulled out his listening device and showed it to Rick. "If you turn both the squelch and the volume controls all the way up, you can flip this switch back here for output. That emits a high-pitched tone that only dogs and rodents can hear. They can't stand it!"

"Hmm." A grin slowly grew across Rick's face. "I like that idea! But it's more than a mile away."

"Lazy!" Tom chided him.

"Of course I am," Rick laughed. "All right, we need a plan. What do you think, Thomas Spencer of the Spencer family detectives?"

"Glad you asked," Tom replied. He took out a pen and a small notebook from the Mustang's center console and drew a map of the junkyard. "Okay, here is the trailer, here are the cars. Right here," he pointed on the map, "is a small tool shed I noticed. The door was just hanging loose in the breeze. We'll hide in there and you can take pictures. Don't bother getting pictures of the old junkers. Just get the newer cars and those pickup trucks that still have wheels on them. See if you can get a snapshot of the guy, too."

"From the tool shed?" Rick asked.

"From the tool shed. We can't risk it anywhere else. I won't be able to listen in because the spy kit will be in ultra-sonic mode. We'll creep up to the shed, take the pictures, and then creep out of there."

"What if we get caught?" Rick asked. "Maybe we should both charge 'em!"

"Nope, too risky," Tom said cooly. "This is scary enough without having to tackle someone! We'll just run like crazy."

"Oh, *that's* a good solution," Rick said sarcastically.

Tom sighed. "You already talked me into this crazy trip, so let's see what we can find out and then get out of here!"

Rick smiled and stuck his thumb up. Tom sighed again, then smiled and stuck his thumb up, too. He turned the car around and drove to the base of the hill. He parked the car behind a large bush.

"Take out all your I.D. in case we get caught," Tom said. "We can use our aliases." Both boys took their wallets out and put them in the trunk. They left their radios and cell phones there as well. The buck knives were the only things in their pockets. Rick brought his camera and Tom brought the spy-listening device without the suction cup or headphones. They each carried a small water bottle with them. Tom walked to the top of the hill, squatted down, and took a long look at the junkyard with his binoculars. He walked back to the car and put the binoculars in the trunk. He silently locked the Mustang, then hid the keys under a small rock near the front driver's side tire. Rick had a puzzled look on his face.

"In case we get caught," Tom said. "I don't want him getting my car keys."

"Oh, brother!" Rick shook his head. They both started walking. They reached the top of the hill and paused when they saw the junkyard. They continued walking along a ditch next to the road so they wouldn't be as visible. They kept walking. Rick began gulping from his water bottle.

"Take it easy," Tom cautioned. "You may need that later." They walked closer and closer to the junkyard. They could see the wrecks at the far end of the dirt lot easily now. Rick felt his heart beating hard and Tom felt butterflies in his stomach. They walked closer. Tom turned on his listening device and switched the rear button to "sonic output." He held it up to his chest. They kept walking until they reached the first car. Both boys crept down. Tom pointed to the tool shed about 200 feet ahead of them. The trailer was ahead of the shed and to the right. If they walked around the left side of the shed, the man probably wouldn't see them, Tom thought.

Tom pointed to the left of the shed and began jogging while still stooped down. Rick followed. About half way to the shed, they could see the dogs. They were whimpering. Both boys riveted their eyes on the trailer as they crept up to the tool shed. Tom finally reached the door and ran in. Rick ran behind him. They pulled the door shut. The boys panted hard as Rick quickly aimed his camera out the shed's splintered wood-frame window.

Suddenly, they heard growling.
The growling grew louder.

Their shirts were dotted with perspiration. Rick snapped pictures of the pickup trucks and the newer foreign cars. He also took a picture of the front of the trailer home.

"How are you doing?" whispered Tom.

"About done," Rick said. Suddenly, they heard growling. The growling grew louder. They heard barking!

"What on earth?" Rick asked in a hoarse voice. Tom looked down at his listening device. The power light was out.

"Oh man!" Tom said. "Quick, give me your camera batteries!"

"Holy cow!" Rick cried. He fumbled with his camera and finally pulled the battery plate off. Both dogs were barking ferociously and scratching their front paws on the shed door.

The trailer door opened and the gruff-looking man waddled out. *He was carrying a shotgun!*

"For heaven's sake, the batteries!" Tom exclaimed.

"I'm getting 'em!"

"Forget it now, there's no time!" Tom gasped. The man kept waddling up to the shed. He jerked the shotgun pump up and it snapped into place so loudly that the boys could hear it over the dogs!

"Let's run for it!" Rick shouted.

"Are you nuts?" Tom yelled. "You'll get shot! Stay here and hide!" One of the dogs jumped up toward the window and Rick could see its snout. The dog barked louder and faster. It scratched at the window.

"Quick, take out your flash card and stuff it in your pants!" Tom said. Rick quickly ejected the flash memory card from his camera and pushed it into his sock. He hid behind a wheelbarrow and quickly put his camera under a rusty coffee can. Tom nudged his listening device behind a bag of cement mix and hid himself behind some rakes the best he could. Suddenly, the door swung wide open and the large man filled the door space. He aimed the shotgun barrel toward the rakes.

"Well, well, lookey here. Get out of there, son!" Tom slowly stood up. The man looked around the shed. He kicked a box over, then kicked the wheelbarrow. "On your feet, boy!" Rick stood up. The dogs were at the man's side, barking and snapping their jaws.

Tom and Rick were caught!

Chapter 10

kidnapped

The man with the shotgun walked backward to the doorway and waved his right arm. Another man came out of the trailer and ran toward the tool shed.

"Take the dogs back, Carlos," the man with the shotgun said. "I caught me a couple snoops."

Carlos squatted down and held the collars of both dogs. He began talking to them and then walked toward some of the junk cars. The dogs followed.

"All right you two, march!" the man with the shotgun ordered Tom and Rick. "And no funny stuff! This gun is real!"

The boys' eyes were wide as saucers as they cautiously walked out of the tool shed. They looked all around and watched the dogs leave with Carlos. The other man waddled behind them.

"Into the trailer," he barked.

Tom and Rick slowly ascended the shaky metal steps to the trailer and walked inside. They looked around. Three other men sat inside the trailer. One of the men kept sliding around in the chair. The other kept sniffling. The boys noticed some very nice electronic equipment that seemed out of place for such a run-down junkyard. They saw a new large-screen television, a complete stereo system, and two brand-new computers.

The boys also noticed the cigarette smoke hanging in the air. Tom and Rick scrunched their noses at the strong, dark stench of lingering cigarettes. Rick tried to stifle a cough as the smoke irritated his throat.

"Well," one of the men sitting in the trailer said slowly to Rick. "Haven't we met before? And who is your friend here?" The man stood up and put his cigarette down.

He was the short man who Rick saw in the bank office!

"I uh, I uh, I don't know you at all," Rick stammered. "What are you talking about?"

"Don't play games with me, kid!" the short man snapped. The man with the shotgun pushed both Tom and Rick.

"Looks like you two have some explaining to do," the man said. He pointed to some chairs around a table. "Sit!"

Tom sat down. Rick remained standing and looked around the trailer. He slowly walked toward the table and stood next to it.

"Sit!" the big man with the shotgun repeated. Rick sat down. The short man walked to the table and stood next to Rick. The man looked at Rick but didn't say anything. The large man with the shotgun unloaded the gun and walked down a hallway.

"What's your name, kid?" the short man finally asked Rick.

"Ken Richards," Rick bluffed.

"Richards. Richards. Let's see… where do you live?"

"In Creekwater."

Carlos walked into the trailer.

"I'm sorry we frightened your dogs, sir," Tom said apologetically. "We didn't mean anything." Carlos glared at both boys and didn't say anything.

"Hey Dillon!" the short man yelled down the hallway. "You frisk these boys or what?"

"Nope, not yet."

The other two men in the trailer stood up immediately. One of them blew cigarette smoke out his mouth like a fire-breathing dragon. "Stand up, both of you!" the short man demanded. The boys both jumped to their feet. The man who kept sliding his back in the chair kept wiggling his shoulders while he stood up. The wiggler reached behind him and pulled out a pistol. He aimed it at the ground. The short man quickly slid his hand into Tom's back pockets, and then checked Rick's. "No funny stuff, got it?" he warned Tom and Rick. He then patted their front pockets. "What do you have in there?"

"Just utility knives, that's all they are," Tom answered.

"Take 'em out and hand 'em over."

The boys quickly extracted the buck knives and placed them on the table in front of them. The sniffling man grabbed the knives.

"They look clean now," the short man said to the other men as he finished patting Tom and Rick's pockets. "Sit down." The boys slowly sat back down. "How 'bout you, what's your name?" the short man asked Tom.

"Sean Thompson," Tom pretended. "I live in Creekwater, too. How about you, sir, what's your name?" The men all looked at each other.

"One of 'em is lying!" the sniffling man said while a short cigarette dangled from his lips. "One of 'em has to be a Spencer."

"A what?" Tom asked.

"How come you two ain't got no I.D. with ya?" hissed the short man.

"We, we don't carry our wallets with us," Tom answered. "Our car won't start, see, and we were basically stranded so we started walking this way." All the men looked at each other. None of them said anything for a few moments. The big man came back from the hallway.

"Look," Rick began rambling, "ah, we were just hoping to find some tools in that shed and then we were going to ask you for some help, but we didn't mean to cause any trouble, we were…"

"Shut up!" bellowed the big man. "Dean, you find out anything 'bout 'em?"

"Not yet," the short man replied. Now Tom and Rick knew three of the men's names: Dean, Dillon, and Carlos. They still didn't know the sniffler and the wiggler.

"Really, if you'll just let us go," Tom pleaded, "we didn't mean to cause any trouble. We'll get out of here."

"What's your name again?" quizzed Dean, the short man.

"Sean Thompson."

"And you?" Dean looked at Rick.

"Ken Richards."

"This is just great," the wiggler groaned. "We got a couple snoops nosing around our operations." He leaned to the right, then to the left while he looked at Dillon, the big man who earlier had the shotgun. "What do ya wanna do with 'em?"

"Lock 'em up. We have to figure this out!"

"I still says one of 'em is lying," snorted the sniffling man. "David said a couple boys and a priest been investigatin' the bank. One of 'em's a Spencer. Works with the police."

Dean began cursing. "Dan, you talk too much!" he shouted.

Now the boys knew another man's name. They also knew that David Switzer is connected to these men.

"What's the big deal?" Dan retorted. "We got 'em now!"

"Obviously that first threat didn't work," Dillon said to Dan. "We have to watch it around these kids."

That first threat. Dan must be the one who sent Dad that e-mail threat, Tom thought to himself.

"Where's your keys?" Dean asked Rick.

"My what? I don't have any keys."

"He was the driver," Dillon pointed to Tom. Dean glared at Tom.

"How come you don't have your car keys with you if your car broke down?"

"Oh!" Tom cried. "I — I must have locked them in the car!"

The wiggling man stomped toward Tom and slapped his face! Tom's lower jaw started to quiver. Then the man turned toward Rick, but he put his arm up. The man swung his fist wide and slammed it down on Rick's head!

"Now," Dillon threatened, "maybe you two will start chirping up if y'all know what's good for ya." He turned toward Tom. "What do you know about Creekwater National Bank?"

"I — look, I'm not sure what you want," Tom choked. "You must have the wrong people. Like I told, um, like I told him," he pointed to Carlos, "we are really sorry we scared your dogs. Can't we go now?"

Dillon sighed loudly. He turned to Carlos. "Take 'em to the rental and lock 'em up!"

Carlos moved toward the boys. "Move!" he ordered. Both boys slowly stood up, their eyes wide open as they looked at the men. "That way!" Carlos pointed down the hallway. The boys began walking. Tom looked inside another room in the trailer as they walked by it. He saw a desk with a computer and some papers. Suddenly, he felt something hard kick him from behind! He lost his balance and fell to the ground.

"Quit leering! Get going!" Carlos commanded. Tom stood up and kept walking. He and Rick saw a back door. They stopped in front of it. "Outside!" Tom opened the door and walked out. Rick and Carlos followed. "There!" Carlos pointed. About 200 feet away was another trailer. They walked to the trailer.

Tom's chin began quivering again. He wondered whether they should have gone on this trip at all. He knew they had to do something to help break this case, but he wanted to be safe at home. He wondered what was the right thing to do while he was forced to walk to the other trailer.

Rick felt horrible. He felt guilty because he talked Tom into coming here, and now they are in trouble. What should they do?

They finally reached the other trailer. Carlos pulled a set of keys from his belt and unlocked the door. "After you, gentlemen," he sneered. Rick glared at Carlos and didn't move. He and Tom looked behind Carlos. "Don't — don't you two try anything funny," Carlos said in a low, shaky voice. "We all have guns and there's no way out of here." Suddenly he pointed to the front door of the trailer and began yelling. "Now get in! Move it!" he hollered. Rick and Tom quickly walked inside. The door slammed behind them and they could hear the lock turning. Rick ran to a window. He saw Carlos walking away from the trailer. Tom looked at the front door, then looked at the doorknob and the deadbolt.

"Keyed," he moaned. "The deadbolt doesn't have a handle. You need a key to get in or out. We're stuck."

Rick sighed. "Let's look around." They walked around inside the small trailer. There was a kitchen, a front room, and a bedroom. That was all. There was no furniture anywhere. They looked in the kitchen cabinets.

"Empty."

"Same here."

The oven was empty and there was no refrigerator. The boys were going to look in the bedroom closet when they heard the deadbolt turning in the front door. Their eyes were riveted on the door. Carlos walked in with Dan, the sniffling man. They held coils of rope!

"Turn 'round, both of you," Carlos ordered in a low voice. "This is for your own good." The boys looked at him and didn't turn around. Rick moved his feet apart and hunched slightly. Dan instantly recognized the fighting position.

"Don't even think about fightin' us, boys," Dan snarled. He looked at Carlos. "I'll get the door if you wanna start on the taller one." Dan sniffled loudly and turned the deadbolt with his key. The boys were locked in. Carlos walked toward Tom.

"Turn around and don't try anything stupid," Carlos said. Tom breathed heavily and turned around. He felt his arms being grabbed and ropes going around his wrists. He felt a hard tug.

"You too, big boy, let's go!" Dan ordered Rick. Rick bit his lower lip and turned around. Soon the rope was pulled tight around him, too. Carlos pulled a rag from his back pocket and wrapped it around Tom's eyes. Tom felt the rag tighten behind his head.

"We don't need those, honest," Rick protested.

"Pipe down!" Dan barked. "Like you really have a choice. Hah!"

Soon both boys were blindfolded and bound hand and foot! They were ordered to sit in the corner of the front room. The boys heard the men walk out of the room and the front door squeak open and slam closed. They heard the deadbolt click.

The boys heard nothing for a whole minute. Another minute, still nothing.

"Tom!" whispered Rick.

"Yeah?" Tom whispered back.

"I think they're both gone."

"There's only one way to find out."

"What's that?" Rick mumbled.

"The kitchen counter. It's one of those older metal ones. Metal!" Tom said out loud.

Rick jerked his head up. Nothing happened. "OK, what about metal?" Rick asked out loud. "Oh wait, I know! These ropes!"

Both boys struggled to their feet and hopped over blindly to where they thought the kitchen was. Tom reached the counter-top first. He turned around and lined up the ropes binding his wrists with the counter edge. He frantically rubbed the ropes against the counter. Rick did the same thing.

"They must have both left," Tom panted.

"Yeah. Oh man, I wonder how long this will take to break these ropes!"

"I don't know, but it's our only chance!"

The boys rubbed frantically for five minutes, then stopped in exhaustion. They started rubbing again. Suddenly, they heard the whoosh of a car driving nearby! Their hearts pounded as they waited for the front door to fling open. A minute went by, but nothing happened.

"Must have been someone else who lives in the area," Tom guessed.

They continued rubbing the ropes against the sharp counter-top edge. They rested every five minutes. After half an hour of work, Tom felt his hands move further apart!

"Rick! Rick, it's working! The rope is getting weaker!"

"Let's keep at it!" Rick huffed.

Soon, Tom's wrists were separated. The ropes broke. He shook his hands vigorously and stretched. He yanked the blind-fold off his face and looked around. He and Rick were the only ones there. He looked out the front windows but no one was near the trailer. He pulled the blindfold off Rick's head.

"Thanks, man," Rick said.

"Hang on, let me look at those ropes." Rick stopped rubbing and turned his back toward Tom. The ropes were almost worn through. There was a large knot on one side.

"Keep going. That knot looks tough," Tom suggested. "You should break through in another minute if I help you. That would be faster than trying to untie that knot. We need to hurry and find a way out of here!"

Rick rubbed vigorously with renewed strength while Tom pushed Rick's ropes hard against the countertop. After another couple minutes, Rick's ropes broke.

"Ah!" Rick sighed in relief. He bent over and began attacking the rope knot around his ankles. Tom frantically worked the rope knot loose around his own ankles, too. After another minute, both boys were completely freed.

"I thought for sure that guy would discover the flash card in my sock!"

"Yeah, good thing you still have it," Tom said. "Maybe we'll get your camera and my spy kit out of that shed another day. For now, let's look at all the windows." He ran to the bedroom. "See anything out there?" he yelled back to Rick.

"Nothing. Those guys must be pretty sure we won't get out."

"There's nothing out these windows either," Tom reported. "This bedroom faces the road. They can't see this side of the trailer from the junkyard. Let's open it up right here, man!"

"Yee-haw! Freedom!" Rick shouted as he ran into the bedroom. Tom slid open the window and pushed hard on the screen. He and Rick knocked the screen out, climbed out the window and looked around.

No one else was outside.

"We need to run that way," Tom pointed, "about a half mile or so away from the road," he continued in a low voice. "Then they won't see us. We can jog back to the car."

Rick didn't say a word. His feet answered Tom as he bolted across the dirt road into the desert wilderness. Tom followed directly behind him.

Both boys looked behind them. The trailer grew smaller and smaller but no one followed them.

"Keep going, man! We need to be way out of sight," Tom urged.

"No problem," Rick wheezed. They kept jogging until they were about a half-mile away. They couldn't see the trailers anymore. "We can turn toward the car now, right?"

"Yeah, should be fine," Tom decided. "Remember, if you can see the junkyard, then they can see us with binoculars. Keep watch while we jog!"

Soon both boys were gasping for breath as they continued jogging the mile back to the area where they parked the car. They were both drenched in sweat when they came upon a hill a few minutes later.

"I think this is where the car is!" Rick panted. The boys stopped and bent over, gasping for breath.

"You're right," Tom said with a wheeze. "I remember that hill stretched out as far as I could see. So this is that same hill. Let's stay here a second, then go for it," Tom recommended. "Oh, when we get close to the car, we should wait and watch it for a minute, in case the junkyard thugs found it."

"Then what do we do?"

"Um... ah, then we will jog back a half mile again, and walk back to town."

"Ugh," Rick groaned. The boys began jogging just to the right of the hill. They slowed down to a brisk walk while they caught their breath, then began jogging again. Suddenly Tom held up his hand. They both stopped.

"I see the road!" Tom gasped in a low voice.

"Yeah," Rick panted. The road was about 300 feet away.

"Let's go up over the hill, so we're on the other side, then we'll jog until we see the car. Then we'll stop and check out the area."

"No problem," Rick agreed. They ran up the hill and down the other side. They continued jogging toward the road, this time to the left of the hill. They both soon recognized a large yellow object behind a large bush.

"My car!" Tom whispered excitedly. "It's still there!" Tom and Rick smiled and stopped jogging.

"Okay, now what are we doing again?" Rick asked.

"Let me go up that hill and I'll look around. If someone sees me and you hear men yelling, then run and hide behind that big bush behind us. Otherwise, we'll both run for the car."

"I don't want you in any more trouble than I've already got you into," Rick objected.

"Don't worry about me. Yeah I'm scared, but don't blame yourself. I agreed to come here, remember? Besides, I'm the one who comes from the detective family," Tom said with a grin.

Rick sighed. "Just don't get caught. I feel bad enough already." Tom got down on his hands and knees and crawled to the top of the hill. He remained hunched down and looked all around. He could see his yellow Mustang below. He looked out at the junkyard in the distance. There were no cars moving. He looked for plumes of dust that would indicate cars driving around. There was no dust. He crawled along the top of the hill, closer to the car. He looked all around the dirt road and the car. No one was there!

Tom ran down the hill and pointed toward the car. Rick raced toward the car and stopped at the trunk. Tom ran to the rock in front of the car and picked it up. His keys were still there!

"Let's go!" Tom cried as he tossed down the rock.

"We need our phones! Open the trunk!"

"No time!" Tom shot back. "Get in now and we'll get 'em out later! They'll discover we're missing any minute now!" Rick ran to the passenger door. Tom disarmed the car and both boys climbed in. Tom started the engine and cranked the wheel. He turned the car around and fought his impulse to stomp the accelerator to the floor.

"Why so slow? Let's blast off, man!"

"I can't leave a plume of dust! They'll see that!" Tom said bitterly.

"Oh, man!" They drove slowly away and gradually picked up speed. Soon Tom was driving fast and eventually reached the main highway! His chin began to quiver and his eyes were wet. Both boys looked behind them, but no one followed them. Tom turned onto the main highway and drove toward Creekwater. He accelerated hard on the highway and drove for 10 minutes at highway speed. He sighed heavily and turned off at the next exit.

"What on earth are you doing, man!" Rick shrieked. "We need to get out of this area!" He looked at Tom and noticed his wet eyes and shaking head.

"I — I can't drive anymore," Tom began sobbing. Rick gazed at Tom and breathed deep.

"Okay. Okay, no problem," he said softly. "I'm sorry."

"It's not your fault," Tom said between sobs. "I need you to take over the wheel for me. Can we trade places?" Tom asked as he pulled over.

"No problem," Rick quickly assented. "Let's hurry though!"

The boys climbed out and ran around the car. Soon Rick was speeding down the highway toward Creekwater. Tom sat in the passenger seat, sniffing softly.

"Um. Um, ah, maybe we should, ah, you know, pray something," Rick suggested.

Tom instantly made the sign of the cross over himself. Rick also signed himself and Tom managed to recite the beginning words of the *Memorare*. Rick listened in silence until Tom started praying a *Hail Mary,* a prayer Rick actually knew. Then they both recited the prayer.

They continued praying for the next few minutes. Soon the highway expanded and they recognized the exit signs for the many roads of eastern Creekwater.

Chapter 11

helicopter ride

Tom composed himself long enough to make a suggestion. "Now that we're in Creekwater, we should pull over and get the phones out of the trunk."

Rick agreed and exited the freeway. They looked behind them to make sure no one followed them. Rick stopped at a traffic signal and then turned into a parking lot. They climbed out of the Mustang and opened the trunk. The boys picked up their cell phones and stepped back into the car. This time, Tom drove. After he entered the freeway, he telephoned his father.

Mr. Spencer was very alarmed at what his son told him. He ordered the boys to drive directly to police headquarters.

"I'll meet you there as soon as I can," sighed Mr. Spencer. "Tom, make sure no one follows you."

"We're making sure, Dad."

"Sergeant Manning will want to take a report from you," Mr. Spencer said into the phone. "I know you both probably want to get home and rest after this, but we need to report this immediately. This will change the police strategy so they may get a little angry with you. Try not to get too upset, okay?"

"Okay Dad!" Tom replied.

They said goodbye and ended the call. Tom breathed heavily. He looked at Rick, then looked at the road again.

"You still have that flash card, right?"

"Yeah, sure do!" Rick hunched over and pulled the card out of his sock. He rubbed it and put it in his pocket.

"Cool!" Tom said. "Dad wants us to drive straight to police headquarters. We have to make a report."

"No problem."

"Problem!" Tom countered. "They aren't going to like this. Not at all."

"Hmm. Well," Rick said, "we'll report everything, like we should. Then we'll just have to explain it. I mean, we had to do something! Right?"

"Don't ask me!" Tom laughed.

A few minutes later the boys reached police headquarters. They climbed out of the car and Tom locked it. Rick looked up at the large three-story building before they started walking across the parking lot.

"Here goes," Rick said nervously.

Once they were inside Sergeant Manning's office, Tom told him what they discovered.

"You found it!" the police sergeant exclaimed. "Tell me about this. Wait, let me get my notes going." He clicked his computer mouse a couple times and began typing. "Go ahead."

Tom explained their drive to the junkyard, their capture, Rick's pictures and their escape. The boys also told the sergeant the names of the men and what they looked like.

"I think one of them is the guy who e-mailed a threat to my dad a few weeks ago," Tom concluded. "One of them said something about the first threat."

"Yeah, and that weird guy who always wiggled funny hit us both," Rick added. "I'd like to clobber him!"

"Too bad he's the only one whose name we don't know," Tom added.

"Is that why you have a red mark?" Sergeant Manning asked. He pointed to Tom's cheek.

"I didn't know he left a mark. Yeah."

"We can get them for assault, too," Sergeant Manning said as he typed. He took a big breath. "You know, the important thing is that you two are okay. But because of what you did, we have to change course. Now we are in a compromised position."

"What do you mean?" Rick asked.

"I mean the car thieves know that we are on to them. We know where they are now. Our department has to move fast to catch them."

"I see," Rick mumbled softly.

Sergeant Manning raised his voice. "Before you boys went off by yourselves and got tangled up in this, we had a wider strategy to tie the bank in with the car thieves. Now we have to make some arrests before these guys run away."

"Um, I'm, I'm sorry about all this, Sergeant," Tom stammered.

The police sergeant took another deep breath. He paused for a moment and then grinned. "Well — in the long run it's probably fine. I have to admit, you two did pretty good detective work." Tom and Rick smiled. "Come on," the sergeant said, "we need to tell this to Chief Roswell."

They went into the police chief's office and recounted their story. The chief was calm but concerned. After the boys explained what happened, Rick gave his flash card to the chief. He plugged it into a card reader attached to his computer. They all looked at the pictures on the computer screen. They were discussing the location of the junkyard trailer when Mr. Spencer walked into the office.

"Dad!"

"Rough day, huh Tom?" Mr. Spencer smiled sympathetically. He looked at the red mark on Tom's face and put his hand on Tom's shoulder.

"How are you, Rick?" Mr. Spencer asked. "Are you holding up okay?"

"I'm fine, Mr. Spencer. I just have a headache."

"We have something for that," Sergeant Manning said. "I'll go get some aspirin."

Meanwhile Mr. Spencer discussed the pictures with Chief Roswell and the boys.

"What do you think, Sam?" Mr. Spencer asked the police chief.

"We need the sheriff to move immediately."

"Good," Mr. Spencer agreed, "we have to have all those guys arrested now because they know they are being watched, right?"

"Right," Chief Roswell answered. He picked up the phone and called the sheriff's office. They need to ask the sheriff for help because Pricklypatch is a different town and the Creekwater Police Department isn't in charge of it. While the chief talked on the phone, Sergeant Manning walked into the room and handed Rick two pills.

A few minutes later Chief Roswell hung up the phone. He looked at Tom, then at Rick. "Well," he said with a grin, "looks like you two boys are going for a helicopter ride. If you want, that is."

"Whoa!"

"Oh, cool!"

The police chief smiled. "Deputy McAlister from the sheriff's office wants you boys to help them identify the men at the junkyard. We don't have enough time to drive there because we need to arrest them immediately. McAlister and his men are on their way there now and we will meet them with EagleEye2."

"EagleEye2?" Rick asked.

"We have two choppers," Sergeant Manning broke in. "We named them EagleEye1 and 2. Number two is up on the roof right now."

"Cool!" Rick exclaimed.

"Can we go now, Dad?" Tom asked his father.

"Sure can," Mr. Spencer replied instantly. "I think this will be good for both of you." Mr. Spencer turned to the police chief. "Sam, I'd like to get Father Spencer's help with the bank again. I want to call him while we're heading to Pricklypatch."

"Absolutely. Fine idea," replied Chief Roswell.

"Rick," Mr. Spencer said, "have you told your mother and father what happened to you yet?"

"No sir. Um, I'll call home and let them know."

The group walked out of the chief's office and jogged up the stairs to the helicopter landing pads on the roof of the building. While they got ready for the helicopter ride, Rick decided to call his father instead of his mother. He took the cell phone from his belt and called his father. He told him about the junkyard. They talked for a while and then Rick hung up the phone.

"How did it go?" Tom asked.

"Dad isn't happy, for sure," Rick groaned. "But he said I can still go up in the helicopter to help the police get those guys. And get this — he said I'm a young adult now and if you Spencers are with me, he will let me decide for myself!"

"Oh wow," Tom gushed.

"Yeah, I'm not used to that," Rick said. "He never treats me like that!"

Meanwhile, Mr. Spencer telephoned Father Spencer and told him about the junkyard and the bank's connection. The priest agreed to help and said he would drive to the bank right away. He wanted to talk to David Switzer and try to find the connection between the bank robbery and the stolen cars.

Chief Roswell discussed a few last-minute details with Sergeant Manning and Mr. Spencer. The police chief walked back downstairs. He needed to stay at the Creekwater Police Department building to manage the case. Sergeant Manning, Mr. Spencer, Tom and Rick climbed up into the helicopter and took their seats. Everyone in the helicopter wore big plastic earmuffs because the engine and the large spinning rotors were so loud.

The helicopter pilot turned around and smiled at Tom and Rick. Soon the engine roar grew even louder and the helicopter shot straight up off the roof. Tom and Rick could feel the pressure in their stomachs as the police building gradually became smaller and smaller below them.

Meanwhile, Father Spencer drove to the bank. He prayed silently as he drove. He wished Switzer would come clean and tell him what the bank has to do with the stolen car ring. He thought about the best way to talk to Switzer. Should he confront him? Or try to ask him a few questions?

There was no more time for the priest's thoughts. He arrived at the bank and quickly parked his car. He walked into the bank and asked for Switzer. The priest discovered that Jim Reed, the bank president, was in the office that day. One of the loan officers quickly introduced the priest to Mr. Reed.

"I'm sure glad you and your family are working on this case, Father," Mr. Reed said with a smile. "I'm afraid I have too many obligations to work from the bank very much. I try to get here about twice a month. David runs the bank on a daily basis."

"Yes," the priest answered, "I noticed that. Actually, I wanted to talk with him, too. By the way, how long have you known Mr. Switzer?"

"Oh, about ten years," answered the bank president. "I hired David about ten years ago as a finance manager, but he's moved up since then."

"I see," the priest said softly. He gazed out one of the windows in Reed's office. "Well," Father Spencer finally said sharply, "I do need to have a chat with Mr. Switzer. It was a pleasure meeting you, sir."

"And you too, Father!" Reed replied. Father Spencer stood up and walked into Switzer's office. They greeted each other and then the priest mentioned the bank payroll.

"I suppose you handle quite a bit around here, yes?" the priest asked.

"You could say I am a doctor of money," Switzer laughed.

Father Spencer stared soberly at Switzer. The priest didn't say anything for a moment. Finally, he spoke in a clear, serious tone. "I am the doctor of your soul."

Switzer stopped smiling. He stared back at the priest and blinked a few times. Finally he cleared his throat. "Yes," he uttered, "well, certainly, that is your profession."

"It must be very hard for a man who has worked all his life to achieve something, isn't it?" the priest said. "It must be hard for someone who has always tried to achieve success. Ah, success. It's always just there, isn't it, Mr. Switzer? Yet, how do we know once we have achieved it? What is success? What is it in a man that drives him — that consumes him — to work, work, work hard, always trying to reach that next level?"

Switzer stared at the priest in stunned silence. Father Spencer continued talking.

"There is something in a man," the priest declared, "like a cancer, that eats away at him and the more he nurses it the worse it gets. It grows instead of dies. Perhaps success is like a drug that seems harmless at first but before you know it, you are hooked. You cannot stop feeding that success drive, at least not from your own power. Oh, pride comes before the fall, as they say. Pride can drive a man to do things he never thought he would have done. It must be very hard for such a man. He tries and he tries, he works all his life, only to be shot down and told to do things that are beneath him. Isn't that so, Mr. Switzer?"

Switzer sighed deeply. "I think you should go now," he muttered. He tapped his fingers on his desk and stared wide-eyed at the priest. Father Spencer probably should have left the office then. He preaches all the virtues on Sunday and he tries to practice them. But now he forgot that prudence was a virtue. He couldn't help it. He certainly would not approve of someone from his parish acting in such an imprudent manner. But he forgot all that and continued speaking to the vice-president.

"But Mr. Switzer," Father Spencer said, "isn't it hard for a proud man who never achieved success — at least in his mind — to take on duties that someone less than him should do?"

"Shut up." Switzer began crumpling up a piece of paper in his right hand.

"It must boil in him like a festering wound," the priest continued relentlessly. "The wound never goes away until a man finally does something about it. What? What does wounded pride do?

First is pride, then resentment and envy, then finally the positive act of the will! The action is revenge, isn't that right?"

Switzer cursed at the priest while his hands trembled. He threw the crumpled paper toward a wastebasket near his desk.

"Mr. Switzer, a powerful man who is granted an enormous amount of trust could abuse that trust in a very big way if he decided on revenge, couldn't he?" Suddenly Switzer's telephone rang. Switzer jerked his head toward the phone and immediately grabbed the receiver.

"This is David," he barked. "What!" he gasped. "When? This morning?... All right.... All right... You are?" Switzer looked up at the priest. "I gotta go," he said into the telephone. He hung up the receiver and wiped the sweat from his forehead.

Father Spencer looked into Switzer's eyes and spoke softly. "A man entrusted with a lot of money could steal that money if he wanted revenge for his wounded pride, couldn't he, Mr. Switzer?"

Switzer's eyes grew wide as saucers. Suddenly he reached over to the briefcase sitting on his desk and slammed it shut. He grabbed it and bolted out of his chair. The empty chair spun around and crashed into the wall behind the desk. Switzer ran out of the office.

Father Spencer leaned back in his chair and sighed heavily. "Saint Matthew," he mumbled, "*ora pro nobis*. Pray for us."

Meanwhile, Tom, Rick, Mr. Spencer, Sergeant Manning, and the helicopter pilot flew into Pricklypatch. Tom and Rick could see the landscape below them. The highway looked like a long line and the cars looked like little moving toys because the boys were so high in the air. Soon they arrived near the junkyard. There were eight sheriff's vehicles involved. The boys saw five patrol cars and a van from the sheriff's office driving toward the junkyard on the dirt road. In the distance, they saw two other vehicles driving toward the junkyard from the other direction.

"Look, Tom!" Rick shouted. "There's that hill where we parked your car!"

The helicopter pilot hovered the chopper over the hill and began talking to Deputy McAlister on the radio. McAlister drove one of the patrol cars heading toward the junkyard.

"We will surround the building and then move in," McAlister's voice crackled from the radio speaker. "First we have to secure it. We have a canine unit with us trained in bait and dart tactics. Can you stand by and give visual assistance?"

"Standing by, over," the helicopter pilot answered into the radio microphone.

A minute went by while McAlister's men parked their cars and positioned themselves near the junkyard. Each deputy quickly put on a helmet and a thick plastic eye shield. They were all dressed in black and they wore thick bulletproof vests.

"EagleEye2, EagleEye2 to McAlister, over," the pilot said into the microphone.

"Copy, EagleEye," McAlister's voice replied from the radio.

"I see dust in the distance, probably from a car," the pilot said.

"Copy. We have two more units heading west."

"That dust is different," Mr. Spencer yelled to the pilot. He pointed to the two patrol cars in the distance, then to the dust in the air farther away.

"Copy," the pilot said into the microphone. "But this dust is farther away from your units. It's getting lighter... vehicle is driving away."

"Copy, EagleEye," McAlister said.

A few seconds later one of the patrol cars left the junkyard and sped away on the dirt road toward the faint dust plume. The other cars began driving slowly toward the junkyard trailer and some of the deputies carrying rifles walked behind the cars. They stayed behind the cars for protection. The junkyard dogs suddenly began barking wildly and ran toward the patrol cars. McAlister waved his hand and two deputies aimed their rifles at the dogs. They fired their rifles and the dogs stopped running. The dogs walked around in circles and then slumped over.

Meanwhile, Tom watched everything happening with binoculars from the helicopter.

"Dad," he shouted, "what did they do to those dogs? It didn't look like real bullets."

"Tranquilizer darts!" Mr. Spencer shouted. "They have dart guns and the darts have something in them that makes the dogs fall asleep."

"We could have used those this morning, man!" Rick yelled over the helicopter noise.

Finally the patrol vehicles reached the front of the trailer. Some of the deputies who were behind the vehicles crouched down and quickly ran to the sides of the trailer. The two other patrol cars that drove from the other direction parked a few feet behind the trailer. There were a couple more deputies lying on top of some of the junk cars. The deputies aimed their rifles toward the trailer. The cars and the van were several yards away from the trailer's front door.

Five deputies quickly ran from behind the cars and crouched behind the sheriff's department van. The van was customized for special use. It has bulletproof glass, an interior roll cage, and extra thick metal paneling. The van drove slowly to the front door while the five deputies walked behind it for protection. The deputies wanted to get as close as they could to the trailer's front door. The van parked six feet away from the door. The five men ran around the van and hunched down near the front door. They each held a rifle.

One of the deputies held his rifle straight up with one hand and slowly grasped the doorknob with his other hand. He turned it. It turned freely so he flung open the door. All five deputies ran into the trailer and began yelling.

"Don't move!"

"Do not move! Saguaro County Sheriff's office!"

The deputies looked around. They split up. Three of them ran down the hallway and two of them walked quickly to the back room.

The trailer was empty!

Chapter 12

bullets from the sky

"McAlister to EagleEye2! EagleEye2, come in!" Deputy McAlister bellowed into the radio.

"Copy, McAlister," the helicopter pilot replied into his radio's microphone.

"The junkyard is empty. No one is here!"

The pilot immediately pushed the throttle. The powerful helicopter surged forward from its hovering position. Tom and Rick were pushed back into their seats by the force of the acceleration.

"We are scouting the area, over," the pilot said.

"Copy, EagleEye," McAlister's voice crackled from the radio speaker.

The helicopter zoomed toward the area where they spotted the dust earlier. While everyone in the helicopter looked down at the landscape, the deputies on the ground hurriedly climbed into their patrol vehicles and sped down the dirt road.

Deputy McAlister picked up his radio microphone. He wanted to talk to the deputy who earlier drove toward the dust cloud.

Every car has a number assigned to it. McAlister's car is B9 and the other car's number is C7.

"Baker Nine, McAlister to Charlie Seven."

"Charlie Seven here, copy," a voice came over the speaker in Deputy McAlister's car.

"What did you find?" McAlister asked.

"Nothing," the officer in the patrol car numbered C7 reported. "I drove around a few miles but the dust went away. There's a couple farms and some equipment around here, but that's all."

McAlister sighed. "Copy." He paused a moment. "The junkyard is abandoned. Keep your eyes open. Over and out."

"Charlie Seven out."

Soon all the patrol cars and the van were driving along the dirt roads near the junkyard, looking for anything unusual. The helicopter flew around the area, also looking for anything unusual.

"This is turning into a wild-goose chase!" fumed Deputy McAlister.

Meanwhile, in the helicopter, Sergeant Manning was frustrated. "We must have missed them by only a couple minutes!"

"Did the boys give you descriptions of the men?" Mr. Spencer shouted over the engine noise.

"Yes. I'll have Chief Roswell put out an all-points bulletin to watch for those men."

While Sergeant Manning radioed the police chief, Tom and Rick looked out the helicopter's windows. Tom watched another plane in the sky. He recognized it as a crop duster, a small airplane that pilots use to swoop down low and drop chemicals on vegetable crops. He waited for it to swoop down.

The crop duster kept flying straight.

Tom looked through his binoculars to see the airplane better. Suddenly, he gasped.

"The crop duster!"

Rick looked at him. "What?" he shouted.

"That crop duster! Dad, the car thieves are in that airplane! Here, take a look!" He pushed the binoculars into his father's hands. Mr. Spencer quickly held the lenses to his face.

"You're right, son! There must be at least four men in that little airplane." He pulled the binoculars from his face. "Sergeant, we found our men!"

The helicopter pilot turned the chopper toward the crop duster. Sergeant Manning radioed Chief Roswell and told him the news. Then the pilot radioed Deputy McAlister and told him about the airplane.

McAlister decided to place one car back at the junkyard and have three cars patrolling the area to look for airplane hangars. He wanted to find the place from where the airplane took off so they could search the cars parked there for evidence.

The other three patrol cars and the van would drive on the roads closest to the crop duster so they could follow it from the ground.

The helicopter flew closer to the crop duster. The pilot was about to radio the nearest airport to tell them about the crop duster. He wanted to ask the airport to radio the little airplane, ordering it to land. Suddenly, everyone in the helicopter felt the aircraft jerk to the right. The pilot noticed a dent that instantly appeared on the side of the helicopter. Then he saw a crack appear in the windshield from the right edge and he watched the crack grow along the length of the windshield. He swerved the helicopter down and to the right, away from the crop duster.

"We're getting shot at!" the pilot screamed.

Tom and Rick grabbed the seats in front of them. Their knuckles turned white and they could feel the pressure in their stomachs as the helicopter banked hard.

"I can't return fire from this angle!" Sergeant Manning yelled. "We need to be on top of them so I can see where the bullets will go. It's too dangerous if we shoot across the sky!"

"EagleEye2 to McAlister!" the pilot barked into the radio microphone.

There was no response.

The pilot then radioed police headquarters. He continued to fly away from the crop duster. Tom managed to look out his

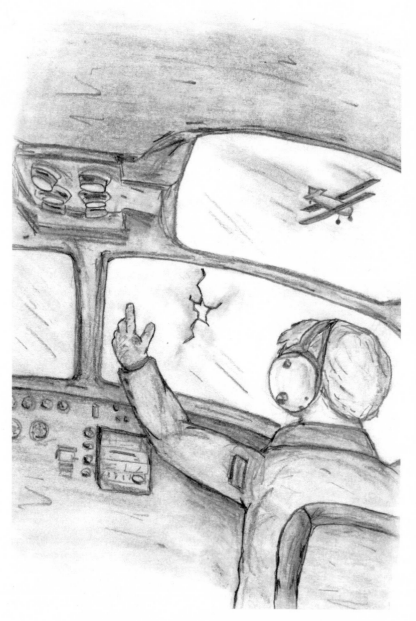

"We're getting shot at!" the pilot screamed.

window while he braced himself. He saw the patrol cars below driving in all directions and he saw a lot of dust.

The police dispatcher informed the Air Force about the situation. The helicopter pilot was told to stay in the sky and follow the crop duster from a distance until Air Force jets could either strike it or force it to land.

The helicopter pilot wanted to talk to Deputy McAlister, who was driving his car on the ground. The pilot tried to radio McAlister again.

"McAlister here, copy," Deputy McAlister huffed into the radio.

"We had enemy fire from the crop duster," the pilot said into the microphone. "Where were you?"

"Getting shot at from the sky, that's where!" McAlister answered.

"We are awaiting jets from Mount Matthew Air Force Base, over," the helicopter pilot assured him.

"Copy. We requested that as well," McAlister said. "No injuries on the ground, but a lot of action. Over."

"Glad to hear no injuries," the pilot replied into the microphone.

Six minutes had passed since the police dispatcher told the Air Force about the crop duster. The boys then noticed two black jets in the distance. The jets grew larger as they flew closer to the helicopter. They flew past at high speed and headed directly toward the crop duster.

"Sergeant," Rick yelled to Sergeant Manning, "what kind of jets are those?"

"F16s!" the police sergeant yelled back.

The helicopter pilot turned his aircraft toward the jets and the crop duster. He flew full throttle until he caught up to the other aircraft. He stayed a safe distance behind the two black jets while the jets surrounded the crop duster. Sergeant Manning reached toward the cockpit in the helicopter and pushed a button on the radio to change the frequency.

"We need to hear what's going on," he said to the pilot. The boys heard different voices on the radio.

"U. S. Air Force. Civil Air Defense to Nine Seven Karen Four, you are ordered to land immediately."

"Nine Seven Karen Four, I can't land, uh, until I finish my rounds."

"Civil Air Defense. Nine Seven Karen Four, your aircraft will be shot down if you do not land *now!*"

Tom and Rick saw the crop duster drop altitude.

"Nine Seven Karen Four, we are landing. Don't shoot. Just don't shoot."

"Dad, is Nine Seven Karen Four the crop duster's call letters?" Tom asked Mr. Spencer.

"Yes. Take a look through your binoculars. You should see the letters on the side of the plane."

Tom looked and saw the letters 97K4 above the crop duster's left wing.

The crop duster flew down toward a dirt road. Deputy McAlister and the other deputies drove on the dirt road to follow the crop duster. The airplane landed on the road. Within seconds McAlister's patrol vehicles were parked on the dirt road behind the airplane. The two Air Force jets circled overhead while the helicopter landed gracefully on the road behind the patrol vehicles. An enormous wall of dust rose up from the ground as the helicopter rotors spun at gale-force speed. The pilot cut the engine.

McAlister barked orders at the airplane's occupants. All the men climbed out of the airplane with their hands up.

Several deputies jogged forward and quickly handcuffed each man.

The car thieves were captured!

When the dust began to settle, everyone climbed out of the helicopter. Sergeant Manning quickly stretched his legs and jogged over to the group of deputies near the airplane. The boys and Mr. Spencer followed. The helicopter pilot stayed near the chopper so he could check the condition of the aircraft.

As Sergeant Manning approached the deputies, he asked for McAlister.

"Which one of you hard-working gentlemen is Deputy McAlister?"

"Right here," a tall, husky, middle-aged man replied. "You must be Sergeant Manning?"

"I am." Sergeant Manning extended his hand. "Excellent work, Deputy!" The police sergeant and the deputy warmly shook hands. McAlister's shirt sleeve tightened as his enormous arm bulged out.

"Oh," Manning continued, "these are the boys you wanted to see. This is Tom Spencer and this is Rick Kline. Boys, meet Deputy McAlister."

"Hello, sir," Tom mumbled and then looked down at the ground.

"Hi, Deputy McAlister," Rick said while he tapped his right foot in the dirt. The boys were afraid of getting into serious trouble because they got tangled up with the car thieves on their own, without asking their parents or the police chief.

"Well, I'm certainly glad to meet you both," McAlister boomed. "I understand that if it weren't for you two, we wouldn't know where these car thieves were."

"Um, well," Tom stammered. He looked at his father, but Mr. Spencer smiled.

"That's right, Deputy," Mr. Spencer replied. "We didn't plan on things working out this way, but Thomas and Rick are amateur sleuths themselves. Do you need the boys to identify the men?"

"Yes, I sure do! First, I want to meet your helicopter pilot. When you talk to someone on the radio, it's always good to meet him in person if you can. Follow me, boys!"

Tom and Rick breathed sighs of relief as they walked behind Deputy McAlister. The deputy and the pilot exchanged greetings. While the men talked, Rick leaned over and whispered in Tom's ear.

"Look at the size of that McAlister guy," Rick hissed. "I'd sure hate to get busted by him if I did something stupid!"

"Aw, you don't have anything to worry about," Tom reassured him with a grin.

After another minute, Deputy McAlister lead the boys to a group of deputies and four handcuffed men sitting at the side of the road.

"Deputy! Sir!" Tom gasped. "There was a fifth man involved!"

"Yeah," Rick added. "Uh, that guy was named Dean. He was at the junkyard. I saw him at the bank, too."

The man who earlier hit the boys sneered at Rick. The man began mouthing silent words to the boys while he wiggled back and forth. One of the deputies noticed.

"Knock it off!" the burly deputy thundered. "None of you will intimidate these boys, is that clear?"

"Aw, we wasn't doing nothin'!" whined Dillon, the big man who earlier had the shotgun.

"Yeah, is crop dusting illegal now? We weren't even doing anything wrong!" said Dan, the sniffling man. He sniffled loudly and began cursing.

The boys told the deputy the names of each man except for the one who hit them: Carlos, the man who took care of the dogs; Dillon, the big man; and Dan, the sniffling man. Soon all four men were cursing and arguing with the deputies. The wiggling man was covered in dust because he wiggled so much while he sat at the side of the dirt road.

One of McAlister's men lit a cigarette while he checked the identification of each junkyard man. The boys got their names right. The deputy also discovered the man who hit the boys is named Joe Nelson. He lives in Pricklypatch. Rick began coughing as the deputy's cigarette smoke wafted toward the boys.

"The dust bother you?" the deputy asked.

"No," Rick said in a raspy voice. He pointed to the deputy's cigarette. "It's not the dust."

"Oh!" the deputy exclaimed. "Old habit. Bad habit, actually. Good thing you don't smoke." He quickly puffed on the cigarette again before dropping it on the ground. The deputy crushed the burning remainder of their conversation with his foot.

Another deputy radioed the names of the junkyard men to the sheriff's office. Meanwhile, Sergeant Manning walked away from the group and radioed Chief Roswell. The police sergeant ended his radio call with the chief and came back to the group a few minutes later.

"I have good news," Sergeant Manning said. "Remember the men who drove to the Neighborly Insurance Agency and looked around the parking lot for their dog?"

"Yeah," Tom answered. "Uh, one of them was named Conrad..."

"The other one was Ed. I remember that guy," Rick added.

"Well," Sergeant Manning said, "George Conrad and Ed Miller are in custody. They were both arrested a half hour ago."

"That's great!"

"Our men arrested Conrad at the bank," Sergeant Manning continued. "There were a lot of reporters at the bank today! Switzer wasn't in but there is a warrant for his arrest."

"Father Spencer was at the bank today," Mr. Spencer said thoughtfully. "I'll call him and see if he knows anything about Switzer."

One of the deputies took out a digital camera and began snapping pictures of the airplane and the four sweaty men in handcuffs.

"Oh, that reminds me!" Rick exclaimed. "Deputy McAlister, can we try to get our stuff back? My camera and Tom's spy kit are in the tool shed at the junkyard."

"Sure, you can ride with me," Deputy McAlister said.

The boys drove with the deputy and discovered that the camera and listening device were exactly where they left them.

McAlister drove the boys back to the helicopter. They climbed up into the helicopter with Sergeant Manning. Mr. Spencer was still pacing back and forth on the dirt road while talking on his cell phone to his brother, Father Spencer.

The helicopter pilot put the oil dipstick back into its place in the engine compartment of the helicopter. He wiped his hands on a piece of cloth.

Everyone was eager to get back to Creekwater.

Chapter 13

barricaded

Mr. Spencer listened closely while he was on the phone with his brother. The priest talked about his meeting with David Switzer.

"John," Father Spencer said into the phone, "I think Switzer could be trying to flee the state. He was really worked up when he stormed out of his office."

"Well, that's not good," Mr. Spencer asserted, "but then again, it pushed Switzer into a corner. So maybe it was good after all. Now he's doing something about it and we have to catch him." The Spencer brothers discussed Switzer for another minute and finished their phone conversation.

Mr. Spencer climbed up into the helicopter where he was greeted by the pilot, Sergeant Manning, Tom, and Rick. Mr. Spencer told Sergeant Manning about Switzer's stressful encounter with Father Spencer. Meanwhile, Tom and Rick were dazzled watching the giant wall of dust fly up from the ground as the enormous helicopter rotors spun furiously into action. A minute later, they were all airborne.

Once the helicopter reached a cruising altitude, Sergeant Manning radioed Chief Roswell and told him about Switzer's hasty exit from the bank. The chief earlier learned the address of Switzer's house from Jim Reed, the bank president.

When the sergeant and the chief finished talking on the radio, Chief Roswell dispatched several squad cars to the Switzer house. He ordered an all-points bulletin to watch for Switzer. The officer in charge of Switzer's arrest was Officer Meyer, who earlier was in the surveillance van with Tom and Rick. Officer Meyer went to the Switzer house with the other officers.

During the flight, the helicopter pilot heard on the radio that the missing fifth junkyard man was captured on the highway! A patrolman stopped Dean for speeding. The patrolman took the man's driver's license and looked up the name on the wireless computer in his patrol car. Tom and Rick got his first name right. The man is Dean Winslow from east Creekwater! The patrolman made an arrest when he discovered Dean's name and description on an all-points bulletin.

Back in Creekwater, six police cars drove to David Switzer's house. Two police cars drove away from the others and turned onto the street behind the house. The house was in a slightly older, upscale section of town. Several homes had large water fountains in their front yards. There were many two-story and L-shaped houses. Most of the houses were made of brick and painted various shades of white or peach. The house next to Switzer's had four large, round ornamental columns holding up its front porch.

Switzer lived alone in his single story L-shaped house. The outside brick walls were painted stark white. There were two large trees in the front yard and several bushes near the front porch.

Four police cars drove slowly down Switzer's shady tree-lined street. Any other day, the shade trees made the street look charming. But today, a hot breeze made the tree leaves jerk back and forth. The crazed shadows from the leaves gave the street a sinister look.

The two cars on the other street behind Switzer's house stopped and the officers climbed out. The other policemen from the four cars parked their cars near Switzer's house. They quickly got out and huddled behind Officer Meyer's squad car.

One of the policemen tried to telephone the Switzer house from a cell phone.

One ring. Switzer looked at the phone, then looked out his front windows. Two rings. Three rings. Switzer stood frozen by the front window. Four rings. The answering machine picked up the call. The officer sighed loudly and pressed the end button on the phone to hang up.

Officer Meyer ordered the officers to split up and surround the house. Two policemen stationed near one of the police cars looked in all the front windows using binoculars. They saw a man moving quickly around the house. He looked like he was packing things into a suitcase. The late afternoon sun hung low in the sky.

Officer Meyer and another policeman walked past the tall, scowling trees and knocked on Switzer's front door. There was no answer. They announced they were from the police department and knocked again. There was still no answer. Meyer tried the doorknob, but it was locked. He stood still for a minute. He looked at the other officer and they both walked back to the squad cars.

Finally, Officer Meyer took out a bullhorn. He announced that Switzer must come out with his hands up. Switzer ran to all the front windows of his house and pulled the curtains closed.

Officer Meyer ordered an evacuation of the two neighboring houses. The low sun cast long shadows as the startled neighbors hurried out of their homes.

Meyer radioed Chief Roswell and asked him to bring a helicopter to the area so they could see things from the air. Roswell immediately thought of EagleEye2 since the Spencers were in it. A minute later, the helicopter pilot received a radio call.

"Base to EagleEye2," a female voice came over the helicopter radio.

"Copy, Base," the helicopter pilot replied to the police dispatcher.

"The chief requests air support for a barricade situation if your passengers are able and willing. Suspect is David Switzer, 8257 North Lakewood Drive."

Tom and Rick both gasped.

"They're trying to get Switzer!" Rick yelled over the engine noise. Mr. Spencer nodded his head vigorously to the pilot. Tom and Rick immediately stuck their right thumbs up. Mr. Spencer grinned.

"Copy, Base, passengers are willing and able," the helicopter pilot said into the radio microphone.

"Copy, EagleEye2. Air support needed for barricaded suspect, 8257 North Lakewood Drive, north central Creekwater," the female dispatcher said.

"Copy, Base, ETA seventeen minutes."

"Copy. Over and out," the dispatcher replied.

Meanwhile, back on the ground, television and newspaper reporters listened to police radio scanners. They learned about the Switzer standoff. Soon reporters and cameramen from all the local television stations and the two major Creekwater newspapers drove to the Switzer house. They began interviewing Officer Meyer.

The police helicopter finally arrived at Switzer's neighborhood. Tom and Rick eagerly looked out the windows and saw six tiny police cars on two streets. From the sky, the large trees looked like plants and the large upscale homes looked like doll houses.

An hour dragged by. Switzer never came out of his house. The police ordered all utilities except telephone service shut off to the house. One of the officers tried calling the Switzer house again, but there was still no answer.

While the helicopter hovered over Switzer's neighborhood, Chief Roswell radioed the helicopter. He wanted to talk to Mr. Spencer, Tom, and Rick. The chief asked the boys to not talk about the shots fired from the crop duster. Roswell didn't want to scare anyone in Pricklypatch.

A few minutes later, Officer Meyer requested a helicopter landing. He wanted the Spencers and Sergeant Manning to help on the ground. The helicopter pilot carefully lowered the aircraft over a large street corner near the Switzer house. The helicopter finally touched down and the pilot cut the engine. The rotors still spun like enormous fan blades for several minutes.

The Spencers, Rick, and Sergeant Manning stepped out of the helicopter and stretched their legs. Immediately, several reporters ran toward them. The reporters began asking questions about the car theft ring and bank robbery. The cameramen carefully balanced their cameras on their shoulders and aimed the lenses at Tom, Rick, and Mr. Spencer. The sun began to set behind the horizon.

"Yes," Mr. Spencer answered one of the reporters, "these are the boys who found the alleged cars thieves."

All the reporters began asking questions at once. Tom and Rick saw five portable microphones instantly shoved under their faces.

"Uh, um, we're both kinda tired, actually," Tom said quietly. He pointed to one of the reporters. "What did you say again?"

The reporter held her microphone under her mouth. "How did you find the cars?" She thrust the microphone under Tom's chin.

"Oh!" Tom replied. "We followed a hunch."

"A hunch. Were you scared at all?"

"Uh…"

"Nah, we weren't scared!" Rick butted in loudly. "We were glad to help the police."

"I'm sorry, but the boys are tired from their ordeal," Mr. Spencer said. "And we have some work to do here. We will give you a press conference tomorrow morning at 11:00 at the Creekwater bank. Tomorrow is Saturday so there won't be any customers at the bank."

"I'll coordinate that with our spokesman," Sergeant Manning added. "We will be there as well to answer your questions. Excuse me, please." He pushed his way through the crowd of reporters and cameramen. Mr. Spencer, Tom, and Rick followed. They walked up to Officer Meyer.

"How's it going?" Sergeant Manning asked him.

"Not good. Switzer is still barricaded in there. I think patience is the key word."

"How long ago did you call him?"

"A half hour ago," Officer Meyer replied. The daylight began to dim as the sunset cast colorful streaks across the western sky.

"Good work. Let's call him again. On second thought, I'll call him. Um, John…"

"Yes?" Mr. Spencer answered.

"If I can't get anywhere with him, can we get your brother over here? He may be able to talk him out," Sergeant Manning speculated.

"I'll ask Father Spencer. It's worth a try!"

The police sergeant telephoned the Switzer house. This time, Switzer answered the phone. He talked with Manning for a few minutes but refused to cooperate with him. Manning began writing a note on a piece of scratch paper while he tried to talk Switzer into giving himself up. He handed the paper to Mr. Spencer. The hastily written note didn't have periods. The paper read:

Call your brother — we can 3-way
have him call me 555-1212

Mr. Spencer immediately took out his cell phone and telephoned Father Spencer. He told the priest what was happening and read the phone number to him. They hung up and Father Spencer dialed Sergeant Manning's number.

The police sergeant pressed a button on his cell phone and quickly talked to the priest. Now he had Switzer on a call and Father Spencer on another call. He pressed another button to connect the man of money and the man of God. Manning listened quietly while Father Spencer said hello to David Switzer. The priest gently informed Switzer that he only had one choice left. He had to come outside and surrender.

The daylight was rapidly vanishing as only the last round tip of the sun could be seen above the horizon.

"Did Sergeant Manning tell you that if you surrender peacefully, it will be easier for you?" Father Spencer asked.

"Yes, Father," Switzer sighed. "He told me. That Meyer fellow said the same thing."

"You have run out of options, my son," the priest said quickly. "It looks like everyone else is in police custody now. You are the only one left." The priest paused for a few seconds. "You know," he continued, "this could be the start of something good for you. Make a decision *now* to come out. It's the first step toward making that pride, that hunger for power, die forever."

Switzer sighed again. The priest could hear him sniffling into the phone. "How did you know? How did you know about those payroll duties and what they did to me?"

"Why, it was simple, Mr. Switzer, once I thought about it," the priest replied. "What might I do if I were tempted like you? It must have torn you up inside." Father Spencer could hear more sniffling. Sergeant Manning kept his mouth covered with his hand and kept holding the phone close to his ear. His eyes were wide as he listened in silence to the conversation. The sun was now completely gone. The entire sky was dark gray.

"Mr. Switzer," the priest insisted, "I want you to hang up this phone right now and walk out your front door. I will visit you this evening and we can talk." The priest heard a big sigh over the phone.

"I'll see you tonight, Father." The phone clicked.

A few seconds later, the front door of Switzer's house opened slowly.

"Watch the door!" Officer Meyer yelled. Several policemen aimed their rifles and handguns at the front door. Two policemen crouched down and jogged toward some bushes in Switzer's front yard.

David Switzer stepped outside.

"Get your hands up! Higher!" Meyer barked into the bullhorn.

The two policemen near the bushes walked toward Switzer and loudly ordered him to lie down on the sidewalk. Switzer slowly got down on his hands and knees and lay flat on the sidewalk. The two policemen ran toward him. Sergeant Manning also ran forward. One of the policemen knelt down and held Switzer's arms down. The other officer quickly snapped handcuffs on Switzer's wrists. Sergeant Manning took Switzer by the arm and helped him up.

"Let's go. Stand up and we'll walk to that car over there," Manning said while he pointed.

"Ugh," Switzer moaned. He stood up as fast as he could and walked with Sergeant Manning toward the police cars in the street. It was dark outside.

Several policemen walked into Switzer's home to gather evidence.

As the officers and the sergeant handled Switzer, Mr. Spencer watched. He sighed loudly and shook his head. He turned toward the boys.

"We'll go home right after this. I think we've all had more than enough for one day."

A few minutes later, the helicopter was in the air again and quickly arrived at police headquarters. Everyone slowly slid out of the aircraft. Tom and Rick said goodnight and ducked into Tom's Mustang. They drove to the Spencer house and ambled out of the car. Mr. Spencer arrived home a minute later. Rick said goodnight to the Spencers and heaved himself with a loud groan up into his father's truck. He drove home.

Mrs. Spencer and all the Spencer children were excited to see Tom and Rick on the television news that evening.

Meanwhile, Father Spencer drove to the downtown police station where they keep all the new prisoners. He parked his car and blinked in the darkness. He walked slowly to the front doors of the large, old building. Once inside, he was greeted by some of the clerks. There were pictures hanging on the walls and a few indoor plants on some of the desks.

A husky prison guard ambled alongside the priest as he was ushered past several security doors and gates. The guard had what looked like a plain white plastic card in his hand. Father Spencer noticed fewer decorations the farther into the building he was taken. Soon the stark, white walls were bare.

The lean priest and the large guard finally came to some cell gates. Each small cell held a prisoner. Two lonely eyes from a prison cell stared blankly at the priest as he walked down the hallway with the burly prison guard. They passed another section of bare white walls.

They slowly walked past another set of prison cells. The forsaken prisoners all stared at the priest. Their empty eyes looked out from their empty souls. Father Spencer and the guard kept walking. They soon passed another section of empty walls and more empty eyes.

Finally the guard stopped in front of a cell. He took the plastic card and quickly swiped it across a panel next to the cell gate. A green light appeared on the panel and the gate made a loud click. Switzer sat alone in the cell. Instead of his usual dress pants and a powerful-looking necktie, he wore a humble orange prison-issued jumpsuit.

"David Switzer," the guard said coldly as he swung open the gate, "you have a visitor." Switzer had already stood up, but when he saw the priest he hung his head down. Father Spencer walked into the cell.

"I have to lock you in here," the guard mentioned to the priest. "Take this remote call button. If you need anything, just press it and we'll come immediately."

"Thank you," Father Spencer replied softly as he looked at the electronic gadget. "We should be just fine." The guard easily pulled the gate closed with one hand. The gate clacked loudly into place and the guard walked away.

"Well," the priest said confidently, "here we are."

Switzer looked up at the priest and didn't say anything for a second. Finally, he muttered. "Yes." He slumped down on the hard, thin mattress in the cell. "Sit down if you want, Father."

They slowly walked past another set of prison cells.

"Yes, I will." The priest sat next to Switzer. The worn-out mattress creaked and groaned loudly under the weight of the two men. Father Spencer sighed and then smiled. "Remember when I told you this could be the start of something new for you? Sometimes men have to hit the bottom, as it were, so God can lift them up."

Switzer sighed in disgust. "Yeah. Rock bottom." He slid his right foot across the floor.

"Mr. Switzer, God wants to lift you up. He wants to heal whatever makes you want to commit these crimes. Your behavior is always up to you, but with God's grace, you can have enormous help! You told me once that you were Catholic."

"Yeah," Switzer answered without looking up. The priest didn't say anything for a few seconds.

"You probably have a pretty good attorney, right?" the priest suddenly asked.

"I certainly do," Switzer said. He turned toward the priest and looked at him. Switzer forgot how gray the priest's hair looked compared to his blue eyes. "I gave the police a report this evening when my attorney was here."

"A report?"

"You know," Switzer continued, "I told them everything. There were two of us involved at the bank, George Conrad and myself. I knew two of the Pricklypatch men from my college days. They dropped out pretty early. Didn't amount to much. I knew they were stealing those cars, and I was so angry at how things were going at the bank. I wanted more power, and then Reed made me do payroll." He sighed loudly. "I wasn't there when the Pricklypatch gang robbed the bank, but I let them do it. I told them where to cut into the roof to get into the vault. I got a hundred grand out of it, but the police already found that money in my house."

Neither man said anything for a few seconds. Finally, Switzer shook his head. "Look at me now. Oh, look at me now. I wanted more power." His chin began to quiver and he buried his face into his hands. Father Spencer reached into his pocket and pulled out a long, skinny piece of fancy linen and hung it around his neck.

"Mr. Switzer," the priest said softly, "tonight you confessed your sins to the government, which only knows how to punish you." The priest looked up at the dirty ceiling, then hung his head down. "Now," he whispered in a raspy voice, "confess to God, who can forgive you!"

The powerful bank executive lifted up his head. His eyes were wet. He looked at the priest and slid off the mattress. He dropped to his knees and began saying words he hadn't said in decades. "Bless me Father, for I have sinned. It's been 30 years since my last confession..."

Meanwhile, on the other side of town, Tom and Rick thought of all the day's events as they prepared for bed. Each one wondered if he would be able to sleep in the midst of so many busy thoughts. But once their tired heads hit their pillows, they both fell fast asleep.

Chapter 14

....

an exciting morning

The next morning, Rick drove his father's noisy truck to the Spencer house. When Michelle heard the rumbling truck engine, she quickly looked in a mirror and ran to the back door. Then she walked casually outside. She squinted and blinked as the bright morning sunshine splashed everywhere.

Rick parked the truck and turned the key to the off position to stop the engine. The engine stopped, then pinged, then coughed, then ran again for a second until it finally stopped for good. Rick slid out of the truck and turned toward a waiting Michelle.

"Good morning!" she sang out.

"Morning," Rick said with a smile. "So what are you up to this fine Saturday?"

"Nothin'. Just hanging here," Michelle said. She looked up at Rick. "What are you doing today?"

"Tom and your dad are taking me to the bank. We have to talk to a bunch of reporters and stuff like that."

"I saw you on the news last night!" Michelle beamed. "You looked great!"

"Thanks. Man, that was a long, long day yesterday!" Rick said.

"So, it's just you and Tom and Dad going today? I'm not doing anything." Michelle hinted.

"Nah, we're bringing your uncle, too," Rick said casually. Neither of them said anything for a second. Michelle looked down at Rick's dirty sneakers.

"I'm not doing anything this morning," she repeated.

"Oh," Rick said slowly. He looked thoughtfully at the driveway. "Maybe you can come with us! That would be awesome!"

"Okay!" She squeaked.

"Let's run inside and ask your dad." They walked toward the house. Rick held the back door open for Michelle as they walked into the family room. As Rick stepped out of the bright sunshine, he squinted hard to adjust his eyes to the room. He said hello to Tom and Mr. and Mrs. Spencer.

"Mr. Spencer," Rick asked, "can we bring Michelle with us? She wants to see the press conference."

"Hey, I wanna go!" Billy blurted out.

"Me too! Where are we going?" Jason asked.

Tom and Rick looked at the younger Spencer boys. Rick sighed while Michelle glared at Billy.

"Well," Mr. Spencer said, "I suppose we could all go there, but Michelle and the boys will have to wait while we talk to the reporters."

While Billy and Jason got ready to go, Mrs. Spencer offered Rick a drink. "Rick, would you like some water or juice?"

"Sure!" Rick said enthusiastically. "Water would be great." Mrs. Spencer prepared a glass of ice water and handed it to him. He started gulping it, but he saw Michelle from the corner of his eye. He drank slower and put the glass down.

A few minutes later, the Spencer family's Chevrolet Suburban was loaded with all the Spencers and Rick. A few miles and traffic lights later, Mr. Spencer turned the large Suburban into the small parking lot of St. Anne's church rectory.

Billy jumped out of the Suburban and ran to the front door. Soon Billy and his uncle, Father Paul Spencer, walked to the Suburban.

"Hello Uncle Paul!" a chorus of young voices sang out.

"Good morning everyone!" The tall, lean priest sang back as he and Billy climbed up into the large, truck-like wagon. "John, before we go," the priest suggested, "let's give everyone in this big truck a morning blessing." The priest immediately raised his hands and spoke some words in Latin. Then he made the sign of the cross with one hand while everyone in the Suburban quickly tapped their foreheads and chests while respectfully making the sign of the cross over themselves.

"Thank you, Father!" Mrs. Spencer said.

They started driving. The Suburban coasted on the freeway a few miles until Mr. Spencer turned onto 42nd Street. He drove toward the bank and finally turned into the parking lot.

Someone in the Suburban whistled.

"Oh, my!" Mrs. Spencer exclaimed. The usually neat bank had long strands of yellow tape around the front doors. The tape had words printed on it that read *Crime Scene — Do Not Cross.*

There was a police car parked near the front of the bank. A couple officers and a man wearing a necktie were standing near the trunk of the car. A large van was parked at the rear of the parking lot. The van had the words "News 11" printed on the side of it.

Mr. Spencer parked the Suburban. Everyone slid out of the truck and began walking toward the police car.

"Hey, look at that!" Jason pointed toward the van. Everyone turned around. A large pole began rising up from the van. Higher and higher it went while a whirring noise came from the van.

"That's a news van, kids," Mr. Spencer noted. "They have enormous antennas so they can broadcast television news from the van." The pole finally stopped.

"That thing must be 50 feet high!" Rick exclaimed.

They walked to the police car. One of the two policemen was Sergeant Manning. Mr. Spencer introduced his family, and

Sergeant Manning introduced Sergeant Kowaski, the spokesman for the police department. He also introduced them to Jim Reed, the bank president.

"Mr. Kowaski has a special job," Sergeant Manning said to the Spencer family and Rick. "He explains things to news reporters. Then everyone can watch TV, listen to the radio, or look at a newspaper or the Internet and learn what the Creekwater Police Department is doing."

"I'd like to bring you all inside to brief you, if you don't mind," Sergeant Kowaski said to the group.

"Sure, that's no problem," Mr. Spencer said. "We have, uh, about 20 minutes before the conference begins."

Everyone walked to the front door. Sergeant Manning removed some of the crime scene tape and they walked inside the bank.

They all sat down in the bank's conference room. The room had a long, wooden table and ten plush, rotating chairs that had caster wheels. Rick, Billy, and Jason swiveled in their chairs.

"Now, who is involved in this? Who will be a part of this conference?" Sergeant Kowaski asked.

"That would be me," Mr. Spencer said, "my son Tom, his friend Rick," Mr. Spencer pointed, "and my brother here, the Reverend Father Paul Spencer. The other members of my family will watch from the sidelines."

"No problem," Sergeant Kowaski responded. He turned to Sergeant Manning. "Did anyone tell them about the air incident over Pricklypatch?"

"Yes," Manning replied. Then he turned to Tom and Rick. "You boys know not to talk about why that crop duster was forced to land, right?"

"Right."

"Yeah."

"Good," Sergeant Kowaski said. "I will discuss the case first, then I will introduce you, Mr. Spencer. You can take it from there. Um, I'd like you all to remember that if you don't know the answer to a question, just say 'I don't know.' I will help you if you want, okay?"

"Okay," Mr. Spencer said.

"Thanks very much," Father Spencer added.

"I guess you talked to Switzer last night, Father?" Sergeant Manning asked.

"Yes," the priest affirmed. His eyes grew wide and he nodded his head triumphantly. "He told me what he told your men last night."

"Did Switzer go to confession?" Tom asked.

"I can't tell you that," the priest answered. "But he did tell the police that he let the junkyard men from Pricklypatch and east Creekwater rob the bank. He even told them where to cut into the roof."

"We recovered about 75 percent of that money, by the way," Sergeant Manning noted. "There was almost $100,000 in Switzer's house, and a little more than $200,000 in the junkyard trailer. Conrad's house had about $60,000 hidden in his bedroom."

The Spencer children gasped. "Whoa!"

"Holy cow!"

"That's incredible!" Rick said.

"Oh, and I have something for you two," Manning said to Tom and Rick. He pulled their two buck knives from his pocket!

"Wow!"

"Thanks, Sergeant Manning!"

"We recovered them from the junkyard," Manning said with a smile.

"I am simply astonished by all of this," Mr. Reed, the bank president said. He rubbed his forehead. "I had no idea David would have done something like this. I knew he wasn't happy with his extra duties, but I had no idea the robbery was an inside job."

"I would like to talk with Tom and Rick alone for a minute, if I may," Father Spencer asked.

"Sure thing, Father," Sergeant Kowaksi smiled. "I'm all done here. Let's all go outside and get ready for the conference."

Tom, Rick, and Father Spencer stayed in their seats while everyone else left the room and walked outside the bank.

The priest then said gravely, "I didn't want to talk about this in front of the younger children, but you should both know that most executives in the business world are perfectly normal people. They are good, hard-working people who obey the law. Mr. Switzer made a bad choice when he let those men rob the bank. Now he has to live with the consequences of his behavior."

"Why did he do it?" Tom asked.

"Well, Mr. Switzer was very upset because he always wanted more power. When he had to start running the payroll program here, he snapped. It's a terrible thing, really."

"What's the big deal with a payroll program? I don't get it," Rick said.

"Ah. That's because payroll is a very important job. However, most executives don't run a payroll program," the priest revealed. "They have accounting clerks who do that for them. Think of it this way: your brother folds the towels and you do other jobs. There's nothing wrong with folding towels, but your parents then make you fold the towels, too."

"Now I get it," Rick said.

"Yeah, me too," Tom added.

"Good. I just wanted you both to know that Mr. Switzer's thirst for power drove him to do this. But most businessmen aren't like that. Oh, one more thing. I think Switzer received a wonderful gift — he saw himself last night as he really is. Most men don't see that clearly very often. He told me he wants to make up for what he did. George Conrad put that knife in your car seat, but Mr. Switzer will pay you back for the damage."

"Oh, cool!" Tom said. "That makes me feel a lot better."

"How come we don't get Conrad to pay for it?" Rick asked.

"Well, son, it's not that easy. Mr. Switzer is eager to make things right, and he will pay for it right away. On the other hand, we would have to force Mr. Conrad to admit to this and pay for it. That could take more than a year if we need a court judgement and a trial. Well!" Father Spencer said with a smile. "Shall we go outside now and join the others?"

The trio stood up and walked outside. There were four large vans parked in the bank lot now. They all had huge antenna poles reaching up to the sky. About ten reporters and cameramen were standing under a shade tree a few feet away from the police car. Mrs. Spencer was sitting with the rest of her family on a large brick planter near the front of the bank.

The two police sergeants walked toward the reporters.

"It's time! Here they come!" one of the cameramen shouted. The group of reporters stood up and walked to the policemen. Six microphones were held up. Four cameras were aimed at the officers and two reporters took small notebooks from their pockets.

"Yesterday," Sergeant Kowaski said into the microphones, "several arrests were made as a result of our investigation into the Creekwater bank robbery. Two bank employees were arrested: David Switzer and George Conrad.

"A vehicle-theft ring was also broken. The vehicle theft operation was based in Pricklypatch and the ringleader was a man named Dillon Danzing. Mr. Danzing operated a salvage business that was a front for the stolen vehicles."

One of the reporters asked a question. "Sergeant, wasn't one of the bank employees a high-level executive?"

"Yes," Sergeant Kowaski answered. "David Switzer was the executive vice-president of the bank. The bank robbery was a conspiracy between the two employees and the Pricklypatch car thieves."

The police spokesman introduced Sergeant Manning as the lead investigator of the case.

Sergeant Manning then began speaking into the microphones. "Approximately 75 percent of the stolen bank money has been recovered," he reported. "The Saguaro County Sheriff's Office also recovered 25 stolen vehicles from the salvage yard in Pricklypatch."

"Sergeant," another reporter asked loudly, "what were all the airplanes doing flying over Pricklypatch yesterday?"

"One of the car thieves owns a crop duster," Sergeant Manning answered. "That airplane was used in the commission of a crime. I can't go into details about that, but the airplane has been impounded."

Two reporters began asking questions at the same time.

Sergeant Manning interrupted them. "Before Sergeant Kowaski and I answer your questions, we would like to introduce a team of private investigators who were instrumental in closing this case. Mr. John Spencer."

Mr. Spencer walked up to the microphones. "I was asked by the Creekwater Police Department to help investigate the bank robbery. My research helped determine that the robbery was an inside job. Ah, I want to introduce some other people who helped us locate the car theft operations. Tom and Rick." Mr. Spencer turned toward the boys. They stepped up to the microphones.

"These are the boys," Mr. Spencer continued, "who discovered the stolen vehicles' location. Tom Spencer and Rick Kline."

"Um," Tom said. "We just kinda, you know, followed a hunch and we found their hideout."

"So, how did you know the cars were stolen?" A reporter asked.

"Oh, we could tell right away. The cars at that hideout were really new looking."

"Yeah, they didn't fit in at all," Rick added. "It was kinda obvious."

"Where were the cars?" the reporter asked. "All we know is they were in Pricklypatch at some salvage place somewhere."

"We found them, um, in a... um," Tom looked at Sergeant Manning. The police sergeant spoke up.

"The boys discovered the cars at that junkyard in Pricklypatch. The yard is on Frontier Road about three miles from the highway. Since the yard was used as a processing center for the stolen vehicles, the property has been impounded by court order."

Sergeant Kowaski then spoke up. "Does anyone have any more questions for the young investigators?" He turned toward the Spencers.

Three reporters started talking at once. Finally one of them was heard above the rest. "I understand that a Catholic priest assisted the police. What role did the priest play in all of this?"

"That's my uncle," Tom said with a smile. Father Spencer stood up and walked over to Tom and Rick. "He helped us figure out stuff. This is Father Paul Spencer."

Two reporters asked the same question. "Do you help the police very often?"

"Only when they can't find anyone smarter," Father Spencer joked.

Everyone began laughing. "You young men must have been pretty excited when you discovered the stolen cars!" one of the reporters said.

"Yeah, we were," Rick said. "Um, we're just glad we could help the police."

Mr. Spencer looked at Sergeant Kowaski and nodded his head. He tapped Tom and Rick on their shoulders.

"Thank you, gentlemen," Sergeant Kowaski said as Mr. Spencer, Tom, Rick, and Father Spencer walked away from the gathering. "I believe the president of Creekwater National Bank has a statement for the press."

Mr. Reed walked up to the microphones and took out a piece of paper. He cleared his throat. "I am Jim Reed," he began. "Creekwater National Bank wants to thank the police department and their investigative friends for their invaluable assistance…"

While Reed read his statement, the Spencers and Rick walked slowly toward Mrs. Spencer and the other Spencer children.

"Well, I guess that about wraps it up," Mr. Spencer said to his wife.

"Hey Dad," Tom said. "I… I want to look inside the bank again. There's one more thing we still haven't figured out."

"Oh? What's that?"

"How those guys could be in the bank office when the desk was covered in dust. It looked like no one was there for months!"

"Go ahead and check it out," Mr. Spencer said. "Ah, tell you what. Why don't you boys look for yourselves? You're getting pretty good at investigating. Your mother and I will stay out here and talk."

Both boys immediately flashed fat grins and skinny thumbs up. Rick winked at Michelle. He tilted his head toward the bank. She stood up and skipped toward him and Tom.

"Let's see," Tom said as the three of them walked into the empty bank building. "This place still gives me the creeps."

"Ah, it's no big deal now!" Rick reassured him.

"Yeah, I know. I guess. You two want to look in Switzer's office? I'll check out that dusty office."

"Let's do it!" Rick answered. "C'mon, Michelle!" He waved his hand. Michelle followed him into David Switzer's office.

"What are we looking for?" Michelle asked.

"Anything weird." Rick opened Switzer's desk drawers. They looked in all the drawers and began looking in the filing cabinets. Suddenly, they heard a cry from the other office! They ran out of Switer's office and found Tom holding an aeresol can.

"I found it!" Tom cried. "It was in one of the filing cabinets. And here's your radio, Rick! I can't believe we didn't think of this before. Novelty dust! Watch." Tom held the can over the desk and pressed the button on top of the can. A shower of dust sprayed out and fell on the desk.

"Whoa! Check that out!" Rick said in awe.

"Novelty dust?" Michelle asked.

"Yeah," her brother Tom said. "It's like those exploding cans of confetti and stuff like that. Party stores sell them. Here, go for it." He tossed the can to Rick. Rick immediately shook the can, held it up in the air and pushed hard on the button. A giant shower of dust descended upon Michelle.

"Hey! Eeeek!" she squealed. "You're getting me all dirty!" She ran out of the room. Rick laughed out loud.

"Oh, I didn't mean nothing." He bounded over toward Michelle and rubbed her head. "Look, Tom, it's snowing dirt!" Michelle and Tom both started laughing, too.

Meanwhile, back outside, Mr. and Mrs. Spencer were discussing the case quietly while the police officers talked to Mr. Reed. Billy and Jason were climbing around the two large planters in front of the bank. The reporters and cameramen were busy putting their cameras and microphones away.

"I didn't get a chance to mention this yet," Mr. Spencer told his wife quietly, "but Sam Roswell offered me a consulting job at police headquarters this week. He wants me to work with them full-time as a private investigator."

Mrs. Spencer's eyes widened. "Really."

"Yup!" He didn't say anything else.

"That's exactly what you wanted!" Mrs. Spencer observed.

Mr. Spencer smiled. "Well, even though Tom is starting college, we paid off the mortgage this year. So I can afford to work at his salary. I'm ready to get out of my technology career and do something else. You and I have been talking about that for a while."

"Yes, that's a perfect fit for you," Mrs. Spencer said. She rested her hand on his arm.

"And," her husband said, "I really want to work with them. You know how much I respect the police and their duties to uphold the law."

Mrs. Spencer looked up at Mr. Spencer. "Did you tell Sergeant Manning that Chief Roswell wants you to work with him?"

"I sure did," Mr. Spencer answered. "Sergeant Manning is a great guy."

Mrs. Spencer smiled at her husband. "You seem to get along well with Sergeant Manning."

"Oh, yes, I do," Mr. Spencer said. "Like I said, he's a great guy. He's an excellent street-tough cop. I think he could tell that

Switzer is a different character than the car thieves. You know, those car thieves, they were a real bad bunch. But Switzer is just power-hungry and he isn't actually violent himself, although he did something really bad. He's a liar, a cheat and a thief — or at least he was until he repented last night — but he isn't violent. His reaction when Paul confronted him wasn't to fight, but to run away." Mr. Spencer sighed heavily, then turned and smiled at his wife.

Mrs. Spencer reached out and hugged her husband.

Meanwhile, Sergeant Manning walked over to Father Spencer.

"Father!" the police sergeant greeted. "I just have to ask you. How did you figure out Switzer's motive? How did you know he wanted to rob his own bank?"

"Ah, my good man," the priest replied with a smile. "It's all simple, once you think about it. You have to think like a criminal. What would I do if I was Mr. Switzer, and I was given those extra banking duties? Why, but for the grace of God, I might have committed far worse crimes than he."

Sergeant Manning opened his mouth but no words came out. His eyes grew wide and refused to blink. Finally, the stunned policeman blinked several times and spoke. "You — you think like a criminal? You, Father?"

"Well of course. Men don't come to you and confess their sins like they do to me. They want to confess to Christ, so they do it through me. It's a sacrament, you know. Oh, we priests learn a lot that way."

Sergeant Manning scratched his head.

"Each person is capable of both good and evil," the priest continued, "Why, people are rarely all good or all bad. It's a choice, Sergeant. Once a man is bad, he can still do some good things even when he decides to commit sins. And when a man is good, he can still choose to do some bad things. Ah, if I was a powerful executive in that position, wouldn't I have the same motive?"

The tough police sergeant didn't say anything. He put his hand under his chin and squinted his eyes. "I — I don't know, Father. I just don't know."

Father Spencer, Tom, and Rick had a great feeling of accomplishment that day. The happy ending to the case of the bank robbery gave them a fresh sense of confidence. They looked forward to whatever great adventure awaited them next.

about the author

Michael Rayes is a native of Arizona and a Catholic father and husband. He is the author of several articles and a past president of three civic and charitable organizations. This is his first children's book. He earned a bachelor's degree in education and has interests in psychology and history. He resides in sunny Arizona where he tries to stay in the shade with his wife, their seven children, and their pet chicken.

Rafka Press

Uplifting Families —
One Book at a Time

112 pages
5½"x 8½" Hardcover
Ages 8 and up
$13.95 US

Tristan's Travels
Karl Bjorn Erickson
Illustrated by Kimberly Erickslon

A seagull afraid to fly?
What would St. Francis of Assisi say?

The misadventures of a timid seagull frightened of nearly everything around him — and afraid to fly! Follow Tristan the seagull, Nipper the not-too-bright squirrel, and Furdock the rabbit as they travel on a rescue mission. Will they overcome their fears? With the help of some animal friends — and help from God and Saint Francis — there's plenty of room for adventure on the journey.

And why does a seagull sound like a rooster?

32 pages
6"x 6" Hardcover
Ages 4 through 8
$11.95 US

Violets for Mary
Norma McCulliss
Illustrated by Sally Bedrosian

Join little Anna and her brother, Joe, as they learn the best way to honor the Blessed Virgin Mary. Walk home from school with them as they learn a lesson about sharing with others. The last day of school is coming soon — what should they do with the rest of their flowers?

This charming new story for early readers will help your child learn to read — and love the Mother of God. Every other page features a beautiful hand-drawn color illustration. The simple vocabulary and short sentences encourage children to read by themselves. The story and illustrations are a completely orthodox presentation of the Catholic Faith for young readers.

Visit our website for more Catholic literature
www.rafkapress.com
602-291-6263

Rafka Press

Uplifting Families —
One Book at a Time

28 Days to Better Behavior
Michael J. Rayes

Preface by Susie Lloyd, author of *Bless Me, Father, For I Have Kids*

HOW TO HAVE ATTENTIVE KIDS AT MASS
AND PEACE IN THE PEW!

110 pages
6"x 9" Softcover
$14.95 US

Worksheets for your parenting style, your child's temperament, where to place the kids in the pew, and more

Focusing strategies for your kids

A week-by-week training plan for better behavior at Mass

Quick tips for better behavior

AND MORE!

Well Adjusted
Michael J. Rayes

34 pages
5½"x 8½" Softcover
$4.95 US

Raising children from hearth to Heaven

Why is it that some children consistently exhibit bad behavior while others tend to be good? The answer: Their social environment. In the debate over nature vs. nurture, this booklet clearly demonstrates that nurture has a profound effect on behavior. Meticulously documented, *Well Adjusted* addresses critical and often forgotten elements of raising children.

Visit our website for more Catholic literature
www.rafkapress.com
602-291-6263